Jack & Diane

Lena Hampton

Cover Art: Canva.com
Cover design: inDEWstyle
Manuscript Edit & Review: Jenn Rosenberger
Copyright © 2013 Lena Hampton
All rights reserved.
ISBN: 978-1-941639-14-6
Second Edition

This is a work of fiction. Names, characters, places, and incidents either are the product of the author's imagination or are used fictitiously, and any resemblance to actual persons, living or dead, business establishments, events, or locales is entirely coincidental.

To Mary for encouraging me to cut up her magazines.

chapter 1

"NO! That ring will never be on my finger again!" Diane's dark blue Volkswagen tore down the state road leading to Indiana University where she was attending law school. The car clipped along, twenty miles over the speed limit. The angrier she got the closer the gas pedal got to the floor.

"It was a mistake. It will never happen again. Haven't you ever made a mistake you wished you could take back?"

"Yes, agreeing to marry you was a huge mistake!" The hurt and the tears had run out fifty miles ago and was replaced with pure anger. That's when she finally answered his hundredth phone call.

"Calling off the engagement and running away like a child is your mistake."

"I am not acting like a child!" she yelled childishly into the phone.

For Thanksgiving Diane had wanted to surprise her fiancée of four months at his apartment in Chicago. She was the one surprised when she walked in on him with one of his fellow resident physicians, making something other than sugar cookies on the kitchen counter of his apartment. All she could do was scream and throw the ring. Her horrible aim was perfect. The ring landed in the garbage disposal, which she promptly turned on.

"This was a mistake, a one-time thing. It'll never happen again," he said, his tone mimicking sincerity.

"I don't know it was a one-time thing. This is just the first time I've caught you, but I suspect it's not the first time you've been unfaithful."

"You have no proof I've ever been unfaithful before."

She noticed he didn't deny cheating previously. "If this is the first or the fiftieth time it doesn't matter. Once is enough for me. If you're cheating during the engagement, why would I expect you'd stay faithful to me once we're married? You would probably cheat during the honeymoon!"

"Maybe I wouldn't cheat if you weren't so strongly protecting your title of last virgin alive." His gentle pleading mode had just run out and he was entering the "my-cheating-was-your-fault" mode.

Diane responded the only way she knew how. She held the phone directly in front of her mouth and screamed then hung up. She threw the phone on the passenger seat and the car was now going fast enough to qualify for pole position at the Indy 500.

A few minutes later her mother's ringtone erupted from her cell phone. After breaking off the engagement, she drove to her parent's house in search of sympathy. Instead she found a mother who wanted her to go back and apologize to Dr. Philanderer and a father who did not want to stand in direct opposition to her mother. Her mother was already upset. If she ignored her calls any longer, she'd be waterboarded and forced into an arranged marriage with Dr. Cheat.

"Diane, Alan just called. He says you will not even let him explain."

"There is no explanation. Anyway, you're my mother. You should be on my side."

"I am on your side. I am thinking of the long term. You need to see reason. Decades from now you and my grandchildren will be grateful I encouraged you to marry Alan."

"Decades from now he'd probably leave me and your grandchildren for the babysitter."

"Nonsense, you will not have a babysitter, you will have a nanny." Her mother stated, not disputing the probability of the future affair.

"Mother, I caught him cheating," she said exasperated.

"He is handsome and successful. Women throw themselves at him and he will not always be able to resist. Men like him cheat, but they always come home. As his wife you will need to forgive him. If necessary, buy jewelry to dull the pain."

Diane thought she would look like Mr. T by their first anniversary. She was trying hard not to do a quick count of her mother's jewelry. It was difficult for her to see her father in the same light as Dr. Insincere. She liked that. She decided Dr. Insincere would be the new name for her former fiancé because that's exactly what he was, someone with an advanced degree in insincerity. Before she could respond the phone emitted its final beep and died. The beep saved her from another insane comment from her mother like advice on picking out a husband's girlfriend.

It hit her, the emotion she was feeling wasn't actually anger or pity, but relief. She wanted to marry because she fell head over heels, not because it looked good on paper. She was finally able to date again and this time she would wait to bring him home. Her mother would not be allowed to hijack her next relationship.

Her mother had grown up poor. She was the first to attend college and graduated with a degree in education and with the all important M-R-S in front of her name. Then the Cosby show came on the air and she saw a doctor and a lawyer as husband and wife and Diane's path was set. When Dr. Insincere came along Diane thought he was cute and he was oh so charming. Her mother saw the medical student as the fulfillment of the Cosby Show destiny she'd planned for her attorney daughter. Her relationship had long passed its expiration date. She stayed because she drank from her mother's Huxtable Kool-Aid.

About three months in Diane was ready to call it quits. Then three years later he was about to start his residency in Chicago and wanted her to move there with him and delay law school. Being a lawyer was the only part of her mother's plan she was excited about and didn't want to give it up. She especially didn't want to give it up for someone she didn't love.

Rolling in the Deep by Adele came on the radio and Diane turned it up as loud as she could. This was the perfect song to sing off key at the top of your lungs in the car while driving away from a breakup. The engine emitted a sudden knock louder than the sound of the radio. The needle on the speedometer was rapidly going down though her foot was increasing pressure on the accelerator. She slowly coasted onto the shoulder of the road.

The phone was lying on the passenger seat dead. It would not even power up long enough to get a text out. One more reason to never forgive Dr. Insincere. He talked her battery dead and now she was stranded on the side of a desolate road, late on the Wednesday before Thanksgiving with no way to communicate. She should have been cuddled up on a couch flipping through one of the many bridal magazines her mother has inundated her with. Picking out a wedding dress was more exciting than the idea of marrying him.

Well, at least the radio still worked. The music would keep her company until a Good Samaritan pulled over and called for help. It was too cold to walk. Plus, she did not really feel comfortable being a woman walking alone along the side of the road. She especially did not feel comfortable being black walking in southern Indiana alone on the side of the road. Just before she went home for break she saw a news story of some idiot passing out the Klu Klux Klan's newspaper on the basis of practicing his first amendment rights. She was fairly certain he had a gun or two to practice his second amendment right too. Those were probably the only amendments he knew because two was as high as he could count. He was probably the odd man out on his thinking, but she did not want to find out she was wrong the hard way.

A half an hour later snow started to fall and her hat and scarf were pulled so close together only her eyes could be seen. It was like a burqa for cold women instead of those maligned because of their gender. Regardless of what anyone says about global warming being fictitious, it being this cold with a chance of large snow accumulations in November proved something.

No cars had passed by her. She frequently checked if the hazard lights were on; they were. She closed her eyes and prayed someone would come along. Preferably a state police officer, make that a female state police officer. This was yet another reason to not forgive Dr. Insincere. Finally, after over an hour of waiting a vehicle pulled up behind her.

It was a big black truck with the spotlights on the top. Was that a gun rack? Yep. And a confederate vanity plate. They say you should not look a gift horse in the mouth, but she was debating which was worse, dying of hypothermia or dying from some torture at the hands of a racist hick. It was a tossup but the guilt Dr. Insincere would have if her body was found frozen on the side of the road had great appeal. Assuming he knows what guilt is.

She said a quick, yet heartfelt prayer this stranger would not do her any harm. She also prayed again for a female state trooper to come along. She cracked the window enough to see and hear, but not enough for a gun barrel to fit through. The eyes looking into her car were such a mesmerizing blue she wasn't afraid at all for a few seconds .

"Hi. Ma'am? Did you need some help?"

The deepness of his voice tickled her ears and warmed her from inside. She pulled the scarf down from her mouth and the hat up to her hairline revealing her face. "No thank you. Someone's on the way," she lied out of fear of her skeleton being found five years from now next to twenty other women who suffered the same fate. "Thank you for stopping sir. It's very kind of you."

WHEN HE HAD WALKED up to the car he was unsure if the driver was a male or a female. The driver was bundled so tightly it was hard to determine, but he hoped a man would choose frostbite over wearing pastel koala bears on a scarf. When she revealed her face there was no doubt she was a woman. A quite beautiful woman with pretty brown eyes and full soft lips.

Snow had begun to accumulate on the window and it was awfully cold. He hoped her help would be here soon. "If you pop the hood, I'll take a look. I'm a mechanic of sorts. Well, I'm pretty good at fixing anyway."

After a few minutes of looking at various things, he returned to her window. She'd unwrapped a little and he could see more of her face. Her skin was smooth and brown like a freshly unwrapped Hershey's bar. "My guess is it's your fuel pump. I can get you a tow and give you a ride."

A look of fear crossed her face. "Thanks for the offer, but someone is on their way. Thanks for looking under the hood. I only know where the wiper fluid goes," she nervously joked and smiled.

He'd never seen anything more inviting than her smile. He smiled and tried hard to think fast on his feet about how to prolong this. He did not believe this was a chance meeting because he did not believe in chance. "Well, I'll wait until your ride comes. Do you want to wait in my truck with me? It's warm."

She stared at him thinking for a long time. "I'm sorry, but I can't. My mother told me not to get into cars with strangers."

His smile made her breath catch. "She sounds like a smart woman. Well, my momma taught me to help a person in need, especially the female persuasion who's beautiful. I'll still wait to be sure you get off safely, but take my jacket to help keep you warm."

He removed his jacket. After a moment of hesitation she rolled the window down just enough for it to squeeze through.

"Thank you."

"You're welcome." He stood looking at her for a tad more than necessary before heading back to his warm truck.

THE JACKET WAS STILL warm from his body and smelled good. It was not the smell of too much expensive cologne like Dr. Insincere. It was a natural, subtle and inviting scent. It smelled like a hug at the end of a long day. After he returned to his truck she realized she should have not accepted the jacket. If he'd returned to his truck with it maybe he'd pull off and someone else would come to help. The cold must be affecting her brain.

The jacket was wrapped tight around her and she felt something with some weight to it in the pocket. Hesitantly she put her hand in, praying it was not a gun. Ration would say it was not heavy enough to be a gun, but a frozen brain does not use ration. The object was a cell phone, a fully charged cell phone. The snow had continued to fall and covered her back windshield.

All her numbers were stored in her dead phone. She didn't even have her AAA card to call for a tow. The only numbers she knew by heart were her parents, Dr. Insincere and the landline for the barely off campus apartment she shared with a roommate. Calling her parents was out for many reasons. Her mother would probably only send help if she agreed to call the calling-off off. Her dad would lecture her on being stranded on the side of the road without a working cell phone. Dr. Insincere was out of the question for obvious reasons. Hopefully, her roommate had not left for the holiday yet. Quickly she dialed the number, but with no luck of an answer.

There was no feeling in her toes and the jacket had lost its warmth, but not its smell. The snow was accumulating quickly. Heat was starting to sound inviting even if it did mean her eventual demise. She had to admit he did seem very polite and nice. Instead of being a comfort to her, it instead made her much more leery of him. The last nice and polite man she met was Dr. Insincere.

When she began to shiver uncontrollably and could no longer feel her fingers, she knew it was decision time. She thought about calling the police, but this was not an emergency. Not trusting her fate to herself she prayed this man, whose name she'd been too scared to get, would get her home safely and had no nefarious intentions. She also prayed he was still there. She couldn't see because all the windows were completely covered with snow. She pressed the numbers 9-1-1 and slipped the phone back into the jacket's pocket.

chapter 2

S NOW FELL ON HER FACE as she opened the car door, but she was too cold to feel any difference. The huge pickup truck was still parked behind her idling. His door popped open as soon as he saw her step out of her car. Carefully he walked to the car.

"To be totally honest with you, my phone's dead, I'm cold and just want this day to be over. I really hope your offer still stands to help me. If you'd drive me to Bloomington, I'd be grateful." The words fell rapidly from her frozen lips.

One dimple appeared when he smiled. "No problem ma'am. I'll get you home in no time. I'll help you to the truck then come back and get your bags."

His beast of a truck was high off the ground. After silently laughing at her futile attempts to get in the truck on her own, he walked closer to help. He put his hands on her waist to lift her into the truck. He lifted her into the truck with ease. He couldn't help noticing the perfect curvature of her denim clad bottom and was impressed.

Gingerly he walked to her car to get her bags. He didn't know much about her other than she was beautiful and very cautious. He was grateful the ride would give them time to get to know each other. Maybe he could even convince her to go on a date. He wondered if she was in a serious relationship.

She sat in the front seat of his truck still cuddled in his jacket. As he put her belongings into the back he'd tried to stop smiling but he couldn't. Normally it would take about forty minutes to get to Bloomington from where her car was, but with the near white out conditions it would take twice as long. Actually the snow was just the explanation he would use for driving so slow. The real reason was he was captivated by her and wanted to extend his time with her as long as possible.

For the first few miles they rode in silence and it was killing him. How could he charm her if she wouldn't talk to him? She probably thought he was crazy with all the looking and smiling. What could he say to her? He didn't know why, but he felt as nervous as a speeding car thief who realized a cop car was behind him. He'd not been this anxious around a female since junior high.

SHE RODE NEXT TO him confused. She felt safe in the warmth of his truck with his smell enveloping her but she was still uncertain of this stranger. His behavior did not match the confederate flag on his front plate. Part of her wanted to stay here as long as she could. Part of her wanted to run as far as she could. It would be about two steps in these conditions. It was in God's hands. Pray and let go was what she was supposed to do.

His voice interrupted her thoughts. "The name's Jack by the way."

"Diane."

He chuckled, "Jack and Diane."

"Yes, Jack and Diane," she said slowly, not understanding what was humorous about their names.

"Like the song."

She looked at him trying to figure out what he was talking about. "Sorry. No clue what song you're talking about," she said, shaking her head.

"John Mellencamp."

"Ahhh," she'd heard of him but wasn't familiar with the song. The car went silent, which was fine with her.

"Do you go to IU?"

"Yes."

"What's your major?"

"I'm in law school."

Diane picked up his iPod and started looking through it. There were many names she did not recognize, probably country artists and some surprising ones. Under the playlist "soul" were artists like Ray Charles, Otis Redding and Stevie Wonder. There were also playlists for classical music and rap. Curiosity really kicked in when she saw "guilty pleasures" it included artist from N*SYNC and Britney Spears, to the Jonas Brothers. Even more confused by her rescuer she glanced over at him. The one dimple in his right cheek had made an appearance again.

"If I show you mine you have to show me yours."

"Excuse me?" she asked throwing her guard back up.

"A person's iPod is like their diary. It's a window into their souls. Since you've seen mine I should get to see yours."

She laughed. The window to his soul was like an M. C. Escher painting. "It would be dangerous for you to look at it while driving. Anyway, my collection isn't as..." her voice trailed off trying to think of a polite word.

"Eclectic."

"I was going to say weirdly random, but we'll go with eclectic."

"I love music of all kinds. I was a musician."

She did not trust people she could not read and he was like Egyptian hieroglyphics before the Rosetta Stone was found. He was handsome, if you went for deep smooth voices, clear blue eyes, stubble and a dimple type. That had never been what floated her boat and she was trying to remind herself of that fact but his dang dimple kept distracting her. Each time he spoke it made every nerve in her body come alive. And it still felt like his hands were on her body helping her into the truck. Maybe she should have stayed in the car and froze.

"Diane?"

"Yes Jack?"

"You seem uneasy. Do I make you uneasy?"

"Why do you think I'm uneasy?"

"You've had one hand on the door the entire time you've been in the truck with me."

She didn't think he had noticed. In her mind she was prepared to throw herself from the fifty foot high truck at the first sign of crazy. It was difficult but she moved her hand onto her lap. "Well, Indiana was never part of the confederacy."

"Come again?" he requested confused.

"Your front vanity plate." She shook her head. "Never mind."

"Please tell me. I really want to know."

"Since Indiana was never part of the confederacy, when I see the confederate flag, especially here, I don't think "black friendly". To me it's a symbol celebrating the not so glorious days of the South, complete with slavery. When you pulled up, friendly and helpful weren't the first things to cross my mind."

His eyebrows furrowed and an unpleasant look crossed his face. The truck slowed down. Without a word he hopped out and went to the truck bed. Then he walked towards her door. She stopped breathing and her heart was racing. She unfastened her seat-belt and slipped her hand into the pocket where the phone was set to call the police. She was ready to climb over the armrest to escape out of his door, but he kept walking. He bent down, the front of the truck blocking him from her view. Moments later she heard the driver side door open.

"The flag doesn't mean those things to me. The plate was a party symbol left over from my misspent youth when I thought I was Bo Duke. I had actually forgotten it was there." He reached the plate out to her. "I am really, really sorry. I never had any bad intentions. I would never want to do you any harm. I hope you accept my apology."

It seemed like he was holding his breath waiting for her to respond. She looked from him to the plate. His apology over a vanity plate held more sincerity than Dr. Insincere had for cheating. Hesitantly she took the plate from him. He continued to look at her expectantly.

"What do you want me to do with this," she asked him. To herself she mumbled, "This is the weirdest gift I've ever received."

"Whatever you want. Toss it out the window. Keep it. Burn it. Whatever makes you happy. I want you to be happy. Do you forgive me?"

She searched his eyes. He was waiting on her answer as if it was life or death. Boy, were his eyes beautiful. They were like the sun reflecting off the Caribbean Ocean. She wanted to go swimming in them. Wait a second. She's not supposed to be swimming in his eyes right now. Just because he removed the plate doesn't mean he's not some kook trying to lull her into a false sense of safety before dropping her in a hole and giving her lotion to keep her skin moisturized like in Silence of the Lambs.

"There's nothing to forgive. Your freedom of speech gives you the right to put whatever you want on the front of your truck." That didn't seem to appease him. "However, you removing it is greatly appreciated," she added.

He smiled a lopsided smile which deepened the dimple on his right cheek. "Thank you."

"No. Thank you for stopping and especially for waiting. I can pay you for your trouble if you stop me at a gas station and get some cash from the ATM."

"Your money's no good here, but if you grab a bite to eat with me I'll consider it payment. You hungry?"

With all the stuff that had been going on she did not realize she hadn't eaten since breakfast. The refrigerator at the apartment was empty because they thought it would be full of thanksgiving care packages. What could it hurt? Maybe she'd have leftovers for tomorrow since everything would be closed on campus and she did not have a car to go anywhere else.

"Okay, but it's my treat. I owe you."

"Sorry, my mother told me to never let a lady pay for a date."

She raised her eyebrows. "Date?"

"Well...I...you know what I meant," he said nervously.

"No I don't. That's why I asked you. Do you see this impromptu dinner as a date?"

"Do you want to be a trial lawyer who makes the witness breakdown in tears and confess on the stand?"

"No, I want to practice contract law. Nice attempt to change the subject, but I'm still expecting an answer to my question. Do you think this dinner is a date?"

He let out a quick laugh which was music to her. "Well Nancy Grace, I did kinda ask you out and you said yes. So I guess yes, this could be considered a date."

"I didn't know I was accepting a date with you. I thought we were just 'grabbing a bite'. A date is slightly deeper. At any rate, I said yes because I don't have any food at my apartment and I won't have transportation to get any until I can get my car towed and fixed."

"Don't worry about getting your car towed. I'll take care of it for you. I can look at it on Friday."

She just looked at him. She was so confused about what was going on. What was his motivation? It's one thing to stop and offer help, but he was truly going above and beyond. She was wondering if she was just a novelty to him. A country boy like him probably had never been with a black girl and he saw this as his opportunity.

When he called it a date she actually felt some excitement followed quickly by forced guilt. She had just broken off her engagement. Dr. Insincere hadn't crossed her mind since Jack's blue eyes peered through her window. Jack intrigued her.

"Penny for your thoughts," she said.

"They're more expensive than a penny."

"What's your price?"

"I'll share my thoughts with you if you'll share what's going on in that pretty head of yours."

"Never mind, that's too expensive for me," she smiled. "Do you think I'm pretty or were you just using a colloquialism?" The question was asked out of curiosity, not vanity.

"I don't go on dates with women who aren't pretty."

"That doesn't answer the question since we're not going on a date," she smiled then bit her lips when she realized she was flirting with him.

"Tonight we're just grabbing a bite to eat. But by the end of dinner you may be asking me out," he said with a wink. They'd reached Bloomington and he pulled into the parking lot of a chain bar and grill. "Is this place okay?" he asked.

She nodded and unlatched her seat belt.

"Wait a second and I'll be around to open the door and help you out."

The hostess escorted them to their table. He took his hat off and a mullet fell out. Her eyes widened when she saw it. She tried not to stare and tried to suppress a laugh by biting her lips. Just when she thought he wasn't a stereotypical hick, along came a mullet.

"What's funny?"

"Nothing."

"Nothing is nothing. It's the hair, right?"

A giggle escaped her mouth before she could clasp her hand over it. "I'm sorry. It's just, well, I'm sorry," she said through laughter. "I'm so sorry, I think it's out of my system now."

"No need to be sorry. I've got a mullet. That's pretty darn amusing to everyone but my mother who thinks it's illegal."

Laughter exploded from her mouth again. It had been a long day and her silly side began to show when she was tired. Normally a person's hair choice was not this funny, but this was her first time she'd seen a mullet up close. It was like she was at a museum looking at the endangered mullet exhibit. He put his old worn ball cap back on and she felt bad. Here she was laughing at him when he'd been so nice. That sobering thought made her reach out and touch his hand.

"I'm sorry. It was rude of me to laugh."

He looked at her hand on his. His hand was warm. He wondered if all her skin was this soft and smooth. She wanted to take hold of his hand and not let go. The thought made her pull her hand away quickly and set it on her lap. She could still feel the warmth of his touch.

His dimple appeared. "It's okay to laugh. That's what you're supposed to do. I lost a bet and my buddy thought this would be funny."

She laughed. "He's not really your friend."

"Oh, I've made him do worse on a lost bet."

"Impossible," she exclaimed on a laugh.

He was quite handsome. His deep voice made her feel something quite inappropriate each time he spoke. He made her laugh. He was generous. As long as the day had been already she wouldn't mind it being longer because she did not want their time together to end. She was really enjoying spending time with him. This thought scared her. Less than an hour ago she was certain he was a racist country boy. She now refuted the racist part but the verdict was still out on the other.

"Can I see your iPod?" he asked, interrupting her thoughts. "Remember, it's only fair since you've seen mine and I'm not driving anymore."

Hesitantly she pulled it out of her purse and handed it over to him. He was right, music preferences are like a window into the soul. She wasn't comfortable with him seeing hers.

He began reading some of the artists and her playlists. He read some of the names aloud, "Adele, Anthony Hamilton, Jill Scott, James Morrison, Stevie Wonder, Robin Thicke, Maroon 5..."

As he read the names she started to wonder if she secretly had a thing for white boys. So secret that she did not even realize it until this moment, sitting across from a pair of blue eyes she was lost in.

"No rap or Hip Hop?"

"Being black doesn't mandate me to listen to certain kinds of music," she said defensively.

"No it doesn't, but being under sixty does. Even my parents listen to some. Heck, even my grandma does."

"You get the Jo Bros off of your iPod before you judge me." She gently ripped her player out of his hands.

"I wasn't judging. I was just curious." He said seriously.

"I listen to some if it's on the radio, but I'm not a big enough fan to buy any. If you must know, my mother didn't allow such "base level music" influencing her children. I never really listened to it. I'm more a top forty with some influence from my daddy's taste for soul and jazz."

"What about country music? You ever listen to it?"

She smiled and raised an eyebrow. "Would it be hypocritical to say I don't listen to that because I'm black?" They both laughed.

"I bet you I can make a country music fan out of you."

"If I lose will I have to grow a mullet?" she said and giggled. He threw a french fry at her as he smiled.

DIANE WALKED INTO THE front door of her apartment. She looked at the clock on the microwave in her kitchenette. It was quite late. She had enjoyed talking with Jack more than she'd expected to and they sat in the booth long after their meal was done. Though she was tired she wanted to feel hot lavender scented water wash away the stress of the day.

An hour later Diane lay in bed and closed her eyes to pray. It had been an eventful day, but she felt blessed that she had made it home safe and sound. She prayed that she would come to forgive the unkind doctor and that her relationship with her mother would be better. Before she said amen, she thanked God for sending Jack to rescue her, even if he was totally not who she asked for.

Despite herself, Diane couldn't fall asleep. Thoughts of Jack kept popping in her head. She'd really enjoyed their dinner together. It was relaxed and easy. They'd talked and laughed until it was almost time for the restaurant to close down. She tried to dismiss it as the rebound effect. The rebound effect is like Cupid's arrow. The first guy you meet after a breakup is always far more perfect in light of the transgressions of your recent ex. Each time she tried to dismiss Jack for all the reasons he was wrong for her, she would think about his dimple, and the way his deep voice tickled her ears, or the way his blue eyes looked at her like she was the prize bike for selling the most Boy Scout popcorn. Her attraction was beyond the physical, he was a gentleman too. Eventually she drifted off to sleep with thoughts of Jack still dancing through her dreams.

SOCIAL NETWORK

Jack Sloan Status: Thank God for foreign cars!
Comments:

Cooper Smith: Your father would shoot you if he heard you say that.

Jack Sloan: Good thing he doesn't get online.

Diane Clark Status: Don't judge a book by its cover, or its mullet.

Comments:

Rebecca Moore: OMG mullets are always guilty as charged!

Andre Stephens: what's wrong with a mullet? I thought it would fast track me to partner.

Ne'Kesha Townsend: Who has a mullet in Gary?

Diane Clark: I'm not in Gary. I'm at school. Apparently Andre has a mullet in Gary.

Ne'Kesha Townsend: I thought it was called a shag on black folks.

Diane Clark Relationship Status: Single

Comments:

Ryan Clark: Please come home so I can have some peace. I can't do this holiday alone. All I've heard is how you hung up on mom. Save me.

Amara Adams: Don't listen to him. As usual he's only thinking of himself.

Noli Freeman: OMG! What happened Princess Di? The engagement's off? I can't believe it.

Ryan Clark: Amara, there's someone else I think about constantly.

Amara Adams: Whatever Ryan Clark.

Diane Clark: @Noli Yes the engagement is off. @Ryan who are you constantly thinking about? I didn't hang up on mom, my phone died.

35 More Comments

chapter 3

EARLY THANKSGIVING EVENING THERE WAS a knock on Diane's door. She paused the TV. A spontaneous smile lit up her face when she saw Jack standing in the hallway with jeans that fit snug on his muscular thighs.

"Hello, Jack."

His crooked smile appeared slow and easy, but he was rendered speechless as his eyes perused her. She was wearing fuzzy knee socks, shorts and a t-shirt. The shorts were itty, bitty, displaying her long legs. From firm smooth thighs to stripe sock clad calves. Her t-shirt was stretched across her round, bra free breast with nipples hardened by the cold outside air that met her when she opened the door.

"Um...hi," was all he could manage from his hormonal brain.

Diane looked down then quickly she crossed her arms over her chest. That didn't help him focus any better because all that did was enhance the cleavage peeking out of the V of her t-shirt.

"It's Thanksgiving. What are you doing here?"

"It's Thanksgiving," he repeated nodding his head. She must think he was a stupid horn-dog with the way he was talking and acting. He looked into her eyes to help him focus and get the blood flowing back to his brain. "I didn't want you to miss out on the holiday so I brought you some food." He stretched his arms out to hand the bags to her.

She opened the door wider instead of taking them. "Would you like to join me?"

He wished she was more readable, but she held her thoughts close to her vest. Was she glad to see him or ready to call the police and get a restraining order? So far none of his normal charms had worked. She was all he could think about but there was no clue if she'd even given him a second thought. She was nice to him, no she was polite to him, but nothing beyond that. He could not tell if she was just being polite or if she really wanted him to join her.

"I didn't call ahead or anything. I wasn't inviting myself over. I just didn't want you to be the only person in the country not eating a good meal today. I'll just set it in the kitchen and be on my way."

"Unless you have other plans, I'd really enjoy your company," Diane offered politely.

"My only plan was to catch a nap while watching football."

"I've been watching Christmas themed romantic comedies all day waiting for the Bears game to come on."

"There are enough Christmas themed chick flicks to fill a day?"

"There's enough for more than a day. Someday I'll torture you and make you watch them with me." She bit her lip as if to trap the words she'd already said. He liked that she was thinking of them in the future even if she didn't intend to share it. Her playful tone was also comforting.

"If I'm with you I don't see how it could be torture."

"Let me go change into something more appropriate for company."

He allowed himself to look at her body once again. "I think you're dressed plenty appropriate."

"You don't think this is kind of revealing?" She raised an eyebrow.

"What it's revealing is mighty nice."

Quickly she walked towards her bedroom. He was somewhat mesmerized by the sway of her bottom as she walked away. The shorts barely covered her perfect backside. He shook his head to rid it of its unseemly thoughts. He needed to play it cool before she ran off like a frightened doe.

He was unpacking the food when she returned wearing a Chicago Bears sweatshirt over a pair of leggings and she'd pulled her hair back into a ponytail.

She was just as cute as she was sexy, and smart as she was funny.

She stopped in her tracks when she saw the feast filling every inch of the counter. "All of that is for me? That's a lot of food."

"I didn't know what you liked so I brought a little of everything. It's Thanksgiving, you're supposed to indulge."

"The scale says I've indulged enough and need to slow down."

"The scale is a liar. You look perfect."

"There's a pie and a cake here!"

"My mom insisted I bring you both. She wanted you to experience the full range of her culinary skills."

"That was awfully nice of her. Wait, you told them about me?"

"Yep."

She waited for him to elaborate but he did not. "What did you tell them about me?"

"Stuff." Again he did not elaborate.

"What kind of stuff?"

"Just Stuff."

"Why are you being so evasive?"

"Cause you're awfully cute when you're flustered, Nancy Grace."

She narrowed her eyes at him playfully at the nickname he gave her. "Are you going to help me eat this?"

"I doubt you'd be able to stop me. The only thing I love more than my momma's cooking is my momma."

They sat on the couch eating and watching football. She was surprised at how good all the food was. She had only had chips and pop so far that day so she had quite an appetite. They both reached for the last piece of turkey at the same time. She hit his fork away with hers. He just smiled and watched her eat it.

"What kind of pie is that?"

"Sweet potato."

"Not pumpkin?"

"She tried to get me to bring one of her legendary pumpkin cheesecakes too."

"That sounds delicious. You're being selfish. I feel you were holding out on me by not bringing it. "

"I was. Plus, I need some leverage to get you to go on a third date with me."

"Third date? You've skipped from zero to three. You can't count."

"You don't know the definition of the word date."

"Just for that, I'm not sharing the pie or cake with you," she said with false indignity.

"I'll be sure to tell momma how selfish you are."

"I'm sure you will since you apparently tell her everything."

She cut a huge wedge of cake and brought the whole pie and a fork back to the couch. She sat the slice of cake on the table and dug into the pie. She moaned with the first bite.

"Thish is sho good," she said with a mouth full of pie.

"I'm glad to see you like to eat. I don't date girls that don't like to eat."

"We're dating?"

"So are you really not going to share?"

"We're dating?" she repeated

"Yep, we're dating Nancy Grace. Last night was our first date and I'm going to go ahead and count this as our second." He said going to the kitchen and returning with a fork of his own and a slightly larger chunk of German chocolate cake that he sat next to hers.

He moved towards the pie with his fork but once again met opposition from her fork. He hit her fork away with his, but she retaliated before he could get a bite of pie. She was quite skillful using her fork as a sword.

TO GET COMFORTABLE HE took off his sweater. As he did so his t-shirt came up a little too, momentarily revealing rippling abs. It was now her turn to ogle him. The t-shirt lay contoured over his pecs and stretched around his biceps. She'd seen something similar before in a museum in Italy, but Michelangelo's David wasn't quite this perfect. He caught her looking and just smiled that cocky little smile that showed his dimple under his facial stubble.

As they sat next to each other his scent wrapped around her. The faint smell of outdoor mixed with his cologne was very masculine and appealed to Diane on a very basic level. The little things about this man were starting to add up to her being attracted to him big time and it bewildered her. She slid away from him so that his pheromones, or whatever, were out of range. She was simultaneously enjoying her body's reaction to him while reprimanding herself for being attracted to him so soon after meeting him.

They sat quietly watching football and binged on delicious cake and pie for a while. Every now and again she would get really excited about a play and jump up to either cheer or jeer at the screen.

"You really get into football."

"My father worked really hard through the week when I was little. Saturday was his day to do yard work or odd things around the house. The best way to spend time with him was on Sunday when he was watching football. My father, brother and I would come home from church, and plant ourselves in front of the TV for the next few hours. He'd even let us stay up late to watch Monday Night Football if the Bears were playing."

"I like dating a girl that likes football."

"Once again, what's this about us dating? We are not dating."

"I didn't say we were. I just said that's a quality I like in a girl I date. But we are dating."

She rolled her eyes at him. Eventually all the food she'd eaten caught up to her and she became drowsy. Her foggy brain did not tell her to stop when she laid her head on his chest. She cuddled into his warmth and fell asleep to the rhythm of his heart beating under her ear. He pulled her in closer and kissed the top of her head, but he did not doze off because he wanted to enjoy the feel of her soft warmth nestled against him.

Slowly she woke to an unfamiliar feeling. Her pillow felt harder than usual. Finally, her drowsy brain reminded her she was on her couch with Jack. Hesitantly she opened her eyes confirming her suspicion that she was not laying on a pillow but on Jack's chest. Even more alarming was that in her sleep her hand had found its way under his t-shirt to rest on the bare skin of his well toned stomach. She yanked her hand from under his shirt and sat up, moving away from him. Of course when she looked at him, he was just smiling that smile at her.

"Sorry. I didn't mean to fall asleep on you," she said flustered.

"No need to be sorry, you were comfortable. I liked it. I like when a girl I'm dating falls asleep on me." Before she could say anything he said, "I know. I know. You don't think we're dating."

Diane hoped that his stomach was the only thing she touched. The fractions of her dream that she could remember had her investigating if his thighs were as muscular as they appeared. She had been engaged to Dr. Insincere and he had never made her feel more than lukewarm. She'd known Jack for a little over twenty-four hours and he already had her hot enough to melt steel. Somewhere deep down inside she felt like less than a woman because of Dr. Insincere's probable perpetual infidelity. Jack made her feel like the most desirable of women and everything he did reminded her how much of a man he was.

Despite the reasons why she was reacting so strongly to Jack, she was going to have to nip it in the bud or at least apply the brakes. He had her so confused she was mixing metaphors. She needed to concentrate on school and her career, not deep voiced smiles. She scooted further away on the couch. Once her car was fixed and returned to her, she would have no contact with him. Of course she would pay for the repairs. Well, her dad would pay for the repairs, but after that she'd forget he existed. A voice in her mind was laughing.

SOCIAL NETWORK

Diane Clark status update: I'm thankful for great food, good football and a new friend. Happy Thanksgiving everyone!

Diane Clark notification: Jack Sloan has sent you a friend request.

Jack Sloan: Today, I'm most thankful for having my momma's great food to share with a new friend.

chapter 4

JACK WOKE UP LATER THAN usual on Friday. For the first time in a while he'd slept soundly through the night. He did not remember exactly what he had dreamt about, but he did remember who they were about. Dreaming of Diane left little room in his mind for the usual stress of his Dad's health. Quickly he got cleaned and dressed to go downstairs and start his day.

He walked into the kitchen to find his Mother cleaning breakfast dishes. He kissed her on the cheek.

"Good morning sweetheart. There's a plate keeping warm for you in the oven. Did you sleep well?" his mother asked.

"I sure did Momma," he said eating a piece of perfectly crisped bacon.

"Does it have anything to do with that Diane you took food to yesterday," his mother asked. He just smiled. "Did she like the food?"

Jack smiled. "You know she loved it. I had to force her to share."

"So, she's no salad eater?"

"No. She has a sweet tooth." A huge smile broke out across his face thinking of her savoring the bites of pie.

"Don't fall for her too fast," she said looking at her son with concern.

"I didn't say I was falling for her."

"You didn't, but your smile did. You've practically picked out the ring and the names of the first three kids. I want you to think through everything."

"Momma, do you have a problem with Diane being African-American?"

"Heck no child, I just hope you're not falling in love with just a pretty face and a nice body again."

"Momma, I don't tend to make the same mistake twice."

"If you say so Jack, I just don't want you to be hurt. Take things slow."

"I'm late getting to work. I don't want Dad to overexert himself."

"Uh-huh," she said to his back.

FRIDAY SEEMED TO TAKE as long to pass as Thursday night did for Diane. And Thursday night took forever with the restless sleep and dreams fueled by memories of earthy masculine scents and steel hard abs.

She was certain that Jack would at least call. It wasn't so much that she was certain. It was more like she was hopeful that he would call. Her intention was to not answer if he did, but she wanted him to call. She wanted to know that his night was as restless as hers. Seven times she'd picked up the phone to call him under the guise of getting an update on her car. Seven times she showed restraint. She knew he'd see through the guise and figure out that she'd been thinking about him. She did not want him to know she'd been thinking of him because she did not want to be thinking of him.

She rationalized that the only reason she was thinking so much about him was because there wasn't anything else to do. She was stuck in her apartment with no transportation. Even if she had her car, where would she go? Everyone was out of town enjoying time with their families. After finding out she had made it home safely, her mother had informed her to call if there was an emergency or she'd come to her senses and was once again engaged to Dr. Insincere. That was no idle statement from her mother, it was a dictate. She knew her mother didn't want her to call for chit chat and end the call abruptly.

Dr. Insincere had not bothered to call either. He'd sent plenty of texts, which she read with the humor she assumed they were sent. 'You're the only woman I love' coming from him surely that was a joke, right? The joke was Diane acting like she wanted that phone to ring with anybody other than Jack.

She was frustrated with herself for hoping he would call. When she was with him she felt...she just felt. Inside there was no longer the feeling of being cold and isolated, instead she felt like giggles, and confetti, and bubbles. Her grandmother would say she was smitten. Her grandmother would have been right. She was smitten with a guy that she'd just met and seemed so very wrong for her. If he was so wrong, why did he feel so right?

Maybe that was just it. Maybe it wasn't that he was wrong for her, but that he felt so right so soon. When she was with him she felt like a totally different person than normal, but seemed so very much like her true self. She did not feel the need to try and be perfect, instead he made her feel like she was absolutely perfect as she was. Dr. Insincere would have been appalled by the getup she had on yesterday. Jack seemed turned on and did not notice (or maybe even liked) the extra pounds Dr. Insincere had insisted she loose before the wedding.

Was Jack really so good or was her former fiancé just that bad? The possible answer was all of the above. It was also possible that she was falling hard and fast for Jack and the landing may not be soft. Diane did what she did best when frustrated, she ran from her problems and into her books. She studied away the rest of her Friday and dreamt of Jack all night.

Saturday morning she tried lounging around watching movies, but her thoughts once again kept going to Jack. Just when she was about to give up on watching TV and call him, her phone buzzed with a new message.

From Jack: Are you hungry?

From Diane: Starved.

From Jack: Good, I'm almost to your place with food.

From Diane: Ok, but please don't text and drive.

Seconds later, instead of her phone buzzing with a response, there was a knock at her door. She looked through the peephole and saw Jack standing there looking more handsome than she remembered. She ran to the bathroom to do a quick check in the mirror. Though she wanted to change out of the old t-shirt and sweats she was in, she didn't want to make him wait.

"Don't worry, I don't text and drive."

"That was quick," she said as she opened the door.

"I figured you're too nice to send me away if I was already here. I brought this just in case." He said raising the bag in his hand. "I figured I could bribe you with more of my momma's food."

She would have let him in if he brought nothing more than a half a stick of beef jerky and a chip bag with just the crumbs. It was his company she was hungry for.

"Bribe accepted. Come on in."

He took a step inside just enough for the door to close from the warming, but still cold weather. "I just wanted to bring you this. I knew you didn't have transportation still and thought you'd enjoy this more than pizza or Chinese."

"Are you always this thoughtful?"

"Yes. I really wanted to see you again too and I didn't have the excuse of your car being fixed yet." He was disappointed that she wasn't wearing shorts again, but she still looked cute.

"Ulterior motives aside, thank you for thinking of me."

"I can't seem to do anything else," he said honestly. "Diane, I like you a lot."

"You barely..."

He put two fingers to her lips. The heat his touch generated left her speechless. "Shhh, don't talk. Just listen. Don't overthink this. Ok?" She shook her head. He looked into her eyes and smiled, nodding until she conceded.

"I know we just met, but there's something about you," he said looking deep into her eyes. "I just want a chance to figure out what it is. Can you give me that chance?"

She nodded her head but said, "I... It's too soon. I was engaged two days ago."

"I'm not asking you to marry me. Just give us a chance to get to know each other."

He was standing close enough that she could feel his heat. His clean masculine scent was causing interference in her brain making it a struggle to think of anything but giving in to whatever he wanted. His eyes had her transfixed so she looked down at her hands that were interlaced to keep from touching him.

"It's too soon Jack. The timing is just not right."

"Maybe it's not your timing, but God's timing."

Her gaze snapped back up to him. He looked serious, which made her smile. "You think God is planning this."

Her smile made his eyes sparkle. "Maybe I do."

"I think the devil has more to do with some of these feelings than God does." She thought back to how his skin felt beneath her hand and the sensations it caused in her.

"You're right. The devil's telling you to run away."

"So it was God that had my hand touching you in not so appropriate ways? Is He responsible for the wholly unholy thoughts I've been having about you?"

"Tell me more about these unholy thoughts about me."

"Jack, focus please."

"I am focusing on the important stuff," he said with a wink flashing that dimple that was becoming her Kryptonite.

"Jack. I am really confused right now. Calling off an engagement to one guy and having uncontrollable, somewhat irrational, and very foreign feelings for another man that I just met have me not knowing up from down. I just need some time to think."

"Okay, that's reasonable. Let me give you something to think about."

He stepped closer. He cupped her soft smooth cheeks in his hard work roughened hands. He looked into her eyes for any sign of resistance, but only saw anticipation and desire. She inhaled deeply just before his lips touched hers. Her lips were soft and warm. He could taste her berry flavored gloss. Involuntarily her hands pressed against the solid warmth of his chest. A low, deep sound came from him at the feel of her hands. She could feel his heart beating faster than hers. Slow and tortuously her hands moved up his chest until her fingers tangled in the curls at his neck.

She pulled him deeper into the kiss. His hands slid down her back until they reached her waist. He pulled her closer. Her soft breasts pressed against him. Another primitive sound escaped him. He knew if he did not stop this now he wouldn't be able to. Slowly he pulled his mouth away from hers. He rested his forehead against hers with his eyes still closed and their bodies still together. Her breaths were rapid and shallow. He wasn't certain that he was breathing at all. He was certain he would do everything in his power to get her.

Her soft voice broke the silence. "Well, that is something to think about."

He kissed her forehead. "Enjoy the food," he said as he left the apartment with a smile on his face. As he closed the door to his truck his phone vibrated with a text message.

From Diane: Here's your one chance. Plan the best date ever for tomorrow.

As soon as she pressed send on the text to Jack she called her friend Amara. As the phone rang, excitement rose in Diane. When her friend answered words erupted from Diane like steam escaping from a kettle that had reached its boiling point. "I kissed a country boy I met two days ago."

"Who is this?" Amara said teasingly.

"It's Diane."

"That's what the caller ID says, but there's no way it's you. Are you drunk? Has Alan's transgressions driven you to drinking?"

"Who?" said genuinely clueless for a moment. Jack had driven Dr. Insincere so far into the recesses of her mind that she had to think about who her friend was referring to. "Jack's the one that's going to drive me to drinking."

"Seriously, are you drunk? Who is Jack?"

Diane filled her in on everything from the car break down to Thanksgiving dinner. "Tonight he drove all this way to bring me food because he knew my only other option was delivery."

"That's nice, in a stalker kind of way."

"If you tasted his mother's cooking, you'd wish he were stalking you."

"My mother can actually cook so I've had good home cooked food on more than just holidays."

Diane laughed because everyone knew how bad a cook her mother was except her mother. "Then he told me he wanted to get to know me and when I said I needed time to think he kissed me to give me something to think about."

"What kind of kiss? A peck on the lips or..."

"The call the fire department and Ripley's because I think I'm about to spontaneously combust kind," Diane interrupted. "We have a date tomorrow. I'm so confused Mara."

"Why are you confused? Some women go a lifetime without being kissed like that. Other's only have memories of being kissed like that by the proverbial one that got away."

"But, Dr. Insincere and I just ended."

"Dr. Insincere? Is that what we're calling him now?"

"His name is not worthy to cross my lips."

"Do you think there's a chance you'll get back with his unworthiness?"

"I don't know why I was engaged to him. I don't even know why I went on a second date with him. I don't think I loved him. I can't even say I liked him."

"I never understood you two either. You looked good together on paper, but in reality something was off."

"What about Jack being white?"

"What about it?"

"I just never saw myself with a white boy, or being part of an interracial couple," she said honestly.

"Don't think of it that way. Think in terms of can you see yourself being happy with him. How do you feel when you're with him?"

"At first I was nervous because I thought he was some racist hick out for kicks. But that changed. Being with him is like, well it's kind of like being with you."

"I knew I got you all hot and bothered."

"I didn't mean like that! I meant being with him is like being with my friend that I've known forever."

"Is he cute?"

"He has these blue eyes and this dimple when he smiles and his clothes keep showing hints of a body that would inspire ancient Greeks. Other than the mullet he's perfect."

"He feels like your friend and there's amazing chemistry, so there's no issue because a mullet can be cut."

"Why did you go into politics? You should have been a therapist."

"Don't worry, you'll receive my invoice in a day or two."

SOCIAL NETWORK

Jack Sloan Status: I love when a plan comes together.

Diane Clark Status: So that's what it feels like to be knocked off your feet. Yowsa!
Comments:
Amara Adams: I like yowsa.
Ryan Clark: I like yowsa too.
Amara Adams: Ryan, if you had yowsa you'd betray it.

Diane Clark is now friends with Jack Sloan.

Diane Clark to Jack Sloan: Thank you for dinner. It was really kind of you.

Comment from Jack Sloan: It was my pleasure. I'll see you tomorrow.

chapter 5

SUNDAY MORNING HE KNOCKED ON her door. Usually she's very punctual, but last night was restless and she did not want to give the bed up this morning. He'd sent her a text telling her what time to be ready for their date, but wouldn't tell her what to wear. She chose jeans and a lavender V-neck sweater as a casual dressy option. The color always looked good against her mocha brown skin.

He was in jeans too, with a baby blue shirt that made his eyes stand out even more than usual. He was also clean shaven. She had grown used to the rough shadow of growth on his face. It was sexy. His smooth skin showed his dimple even more. That was sexy too. Something was different about him.

"You cut your hair."

"I figured there were no mullets on your perfect date."

"What about your bet?"

"I'm sure he'll make me suffer, but messing up this date with you was a steeper price than I was willing to pay."

She quickly threw on a pair of brown boots with a wedge heel that made him tower over her just a little less and glossed her lips. He unconsciously licked his lips remembering the taste of that gloss. He liked that she did not put on a mask of makeup. She did not need makeup to be beautiful. Her large brown eyes were framed with naturally long eyelashes that were soft without thick black mascara.

"I wanted to start the day at church."

"I should maybe change." She turned towards her room.

He took her hand to stop her. "You're dressed just fine. I've been to this church before. You may even be a little fancy." She grabbed her purse and let her hand stay in his. It felt both natural and comfortable, and exhilarating at the same time.

She was surprised that during the service he knew many of the songs the praise band was singing and sang along in a smooth baritone voice. Diane would have never planned a date at a church, but this was perfect. Knowing he had a relationship with the Lord made him even more attractive. During service, he reached over and took her hand in his.

The sermon was about God doing things in His perfect time. Sometimes we needed to be patient and wait for His time to come and other times we needed to hurry up and jump on board because God had the train leaving the station sooner than we would like. They were greeted by a few worshipers after service and invited back.

"Did you know what the sermon topic was today?" Diane asked because she did not think he could have planned it that way, but found it peculiar that it was right in line with what he'd said to her yesterday.

"I didn't."

"Well, that's some coincidence that you just said us meeting was God's timing."

"There's no such thing as coincidences. There are only God instances." He turned to her in the truck. "The day I met you I'd been driving going nowhere, just driving and listening to music and thinking. I had just turned around to head back home when a song called "God Gave Me You" came on the radio. I prayed that he would give me someone. No sooner than I'd finished that prayer, I saw your car. Now, it could all be a huge coincidence that your car broke down in that exact place at that exact time that I was randomly out for a drive and heard that song and prayed that prayer. It could be just chance, but that's a whole lot of chance."

She did not say anything when he finished talking. He could not read her face either. Though she was looking at him, he could tell that she was thinking something. He was afraid he had said too much and she was thinking he was crazy. She turned and looked out the side window.

"You ever wonder why I was headed back to school to be alone on the evening before Thanksgiving?"

"I wondered, but I figured you had your reasons but I didn't know you well enough to ask."

"Uncharacteristically, on the spur of the moment, I decided to go surprise my fiancée in Chicago before spending the holiday with my family. I was surprised by him with another woman. When my mother encouraged me to return to him and work things out instead of providing me a shoulder to cry on, I decided to come back to school and study. My ex's and mother's repeated texts and calls ran my battery down."

She turned back to look at him. "I'd waited for quite some time without a single car passing me by so I prayed God would send me some help before I froze to death. When I opened my eyes, you were getting out of your truck and headed my way."

That was a lot of information for him to take in and he thought she still had more to say so he stayed silent. She was quiet too, lost in her thoughts.

"You have a valid argument. Those are quite a few coincidences. It would seem that we were meant to meet but it doesn't mean we were meant to be together."

"You're right, but I think this is a strong argument that we are supposed to be together." He kissed her again. It was a brief brush of his lips on hers.

"You really need to stop doing that brain scrambling thing to me."

"You mean kiss you?"

She pointed at him nodding. "Exactly. That thing."

"Darlin', I'd have to go to rehab to stop that." He put another quick kiss on her lips to emphasize his point.

"Coincidences and kisses aren't enough to build a relationship on."

"Diane, I'm not saying marry me before the night is done. I'm just hoping you won't turn me into a pumpkin at the stroke of midnight."

"That's not how that goes."

"Details," he reached into the extended cab of his truck and brought out a simply wrapped box. "This is for you. You'll need it for the next part of our date."

She unwrapped it nervously. It was too soon for gifts. Her mind was racing trying to figure out what he'd gotten her. Blankly she stared at the content of the box then began to smile. "Thank you," she said holding a Colts sweatshirt to her.

"I know you're a Bears fan, but I was hoping you'd route for the Colts with me today."

"Of course. I'm a Colts fan too. They're my AFC team, but Da Bears are first in my heart."

"Someday I want to be first in your heart."

"I think maybe someday you could be." When she saw his smile broaden she realized that she said it out loud and did not just think it. She was nervous because not only did she mean it, but she knew deep down that he may already be. Falling fast usually means landing hard. She laughed to brush her fear aside. "Was that a sufficiently cheesy response to your corny line?"

He saw the fear flash in her eyes so he used humor to defuse it. "It may have been corny, but admit you liked it."

"I will admit to no such thing."

"Feel free to change right here in front of me. I won't look," he said, putting his hands over his eyes with his fingers spread apart.

She did not respond verbally but instead surprised him by beginning to take her sweater off. He was excited as she began to pull her sweater up until he saw the t-shirt she was wearing underneath it. He was still rewarded because the V-neck of her t-shirt was deep and revealed some cleavage that the sweater hadn't. As she pulled the sweater over her head, her t-shirt came up an inch or two, revealing the smooth brown skin of her stomach. His eyes were transfixed on her. He was enjoying this flirty side of her, but he thought it may be the death of him as he could feel his heart beating harder.

He then pulled another Colts' jersey from the back. Jack pulled his shirt off revealing his bare chest. Diane held her breath at the sight of his stomach. His abs were perfectly rippled like sand that had been blown by the wind. She let out a breath slowly. Her fingers tickled with desire to reach out and touch him again. He pulled on a t-shirt and smoothed it out far more than necessary. He pulled the jersey over his head and started the truck as though what he'd done had not been intended to raise her blood pressure.

They went and watched football together. Her passion for the game excited him almost as much as her passion for greasy bar food. Something had changed. The wall she'd had up was down and she was fully the person she'd only shown glimpses of before. She'd even drank a beer. The more time they spent together, the more they surprised each other in good ways. When the game was over they stayed and talked.

"This was a great date Jack," she said as they walked to his truck outside of the bar.

"It's not over yet. The best is still to come, unless you're tired."

"There's more? There's not going to be anything left for a second date."

"You told me this was my one chance. I planned like there may not be a second date."

"There may not be." She smiled at him. "So, what's next?"

"Just wait and see."

He drove for what seemed like forever. Four days ago she sat in a broken down car in front of this truck freaked the freak out that he was going to brutalize her. Despite her growing attraction to him, there was still the thought in the back of her head that this was all part of some evil plan. The deeper they drove into nowhere Indiana, the more she believed this to be true. There was a small part of her that just wanted to drive with Jack in this truck all night. He reached out and took her hand, bringing it to his lips to brush a kiss across it then returning their entwined hands to the center console. They drove hand in hand quietly for a little while longer.

He turned the truck off the road and into a harvested field. Two factions of nervous butterflies warred in her stomach as her body was feeling a physical attraction she wasn't certain she could control and her mind was considering various possibilities of impending peril. They drove far enough into the field that any direction you looked you just saw more field. He pointed to the truck so that the bed was facing west.

"Where are we?"

"This is my farm. Well, it's my family's farm."

"What are we doing here?"

"I brought you to watch the sunset. Have you ever seen a clear sunset?"

"I don't think I've ever watched the sunset. I've seen it set, but not on purpose, usually it was just an outcome of driving west in the evening."

He pulled a cooler out of the extended cab then walked around to help her out. Every time he helped her down out of the truck he did it so that her body would have to slide next to his. He let down the tailgate. He attempted to help her up but she motioned that she could do it on her own. If he touched her one more time she thought she'd melt into a puddle of hormones under a sexy smelling sweatshirt. He was disappointed he did not get the opportunity to touch her again, but he received the reward of watching her lovely backside as she momentarily struggled to get up on the tailgate. With ease he hopped onto it and sat next to her.

"Is this a normal first date out of the Jack playboy playbook?"

"Why do you think I'm a playboy?"

"You're far too charming not to be."

"So, you think I'm charming?" he said with a smile.

"Yes, but it's far from a compliment." She laughed.

His smile broadened at the lilt of her laughter. "This is not a normal first date for me. I wanted as much opportunity as possible for us to get to know each other. FYI, players don't take dates to church."

"Oh but they do. It's all part of throwing unsuspecting women off their scent." He just smiled in response. "How does one watch the sunset? Do you just look west and wait to see if it goes down or maybe even wait to see if it will surprise you and go back up?"

He sat the cooler next to her and headed back to the cab of the truck. He grabbed his iPod, a pillow and a couple of blankets from the back. When he returned to the back of the truck she was lifting a forkful of cheesecake to her perfect mouth. She paused like a child does when their mother finds them eating from her private stash of candy. Watching her eat was a sensual experience. When she enjoyed what she was eating her face had the same look as it does just after they kiss.

He hopped up onto the tailgate like a pro. He put one of the blankets down on the bed of the truck and propped the pillow up against the side. He took a seat. "I have some songs I want you to listen to."

"Is this part of your attempted conversion to country?" She scooted the other pillow a little further away from him and sat down.

"It's not a conversion attempt. I just want you to give it a chance." He had a headphone splitter and two pairs of headphones. He handed one set to her. He was crafty because she had to scoot back next to him, even closer than she was originally, for the headphones to reach.

"The first song isn't country, but since you didn't get my reference the other day I thought I'd play 'Jack and Diane' for you."

After the Mellencamp song there were drums followed by the twang of a guitar or banjo then a deep baritone similar to Jack's began to sing. Then a different voice began to sing. It seemed familiar. Recognition dawned on her and she looked at Jack with her bright brown eyes.

"Is that Anthony Hamilton?"

"It sure is." He smiled at her. "He's singing with Josh Turner."

They sat listening to music as the sun dipped below the horizon. The sky was alight with hues of purple, blue, peach and orange. There were still remnants of snow that had survived the unseasonable rise in temperature since the holiday.

As they listened to more songs by many of the names she did not recognize on his iPod she moved closer to his warmth as it grew cooler without the warmth of the sun. The gentle rhythms of the music and soothing vocals about love wound a spell around her. She leaned into him and he took her hand into his. With each song that played he told her who it was and would interject musical knowledge into it.

"This is the song that I heard just before I met you."

"I've heard that song before. A different version though, on the contemporary Christian station I listen to sometimes."

"Dave Barnes did it last year."

"You know a lot about music."

He sat quietly for a moment and looked out over the horizon. "I had a record deal once."

She waited for him to elaborate, but he did not. He seemed lost in thought. "What happened?"

"It's a long story. I don't want to bore you."

"You don't have to tell me if you don't want to." She was disappointed that he did not want to tell her. Without thinking she pulled her hand from his.

He could feel their emotional closeness change with the physical distance. He wrapped his arm around her and pulled her back into him. She came easily without a fight because that's where she wanted to be.

"When I graduated from high school I moved to Nashville with dreams of becoming the next big thing. I worked odd jobs and played any gig that came along. After about two years I finally caught a break and started getting into some better places. I was writing and even had a couple of songs recorded by major artists. A manager of one of the artists liked my voice and started representing me. About a year later I had a contract. Halfway through writing songs for the album I got a call from my momma saying that my dad was sick. She could not take care of him and the farm so I came home to help and I've been here ever since."

"You gave up a lot. You gave up what you love."

"No, I gave up my passion. What I love is my parents and this farm. Passion is something that has the tendency to burn out, but love can burn forever. I knew if I didn't come back it would only be a matter of time before the farm would have to be sold. It's been in our family forever and I didn't want some pipe dream of mine to be what ended the legacy. Having a record contract doesn't guarantee success. Looking back, it was likely for the best.""Why is that?"

"Young and stupid was the best way to describe me. I was partying way too hard with no fame and a little money. If I had hit it big then I wouldn't have handled it well. Money and fame would have been like striking a match to gasoline drenched TNT."

"Were you doing drugs?"

"No, but Jack, Jim, and Jose were good friends."

"Who are they?"

"Jack Daniels, Jim Beam, and Jose Cuervo."

"Were you an alcoholic?"

"No, but the hard stuff makes me stupid. Some of my worst decisions were made after a night with any one of those three."

"What was wrong with your father?"

"Cancer. After surgery and chemo it went into remission for a while."

"A while? Did it come back?"

"Last month, his doctor found a tumor. They aren't sure that it's cancerous. He has a biopsy scheduled for after the holidays."

"Jack. I'm so sorry to hear that." He went quiet again. She could tell how much his father's illness bothered him. "I didn't know there were this many stars in the sky. It's beautiful. Thank you for bringing me out here."

"You're beautiful Diane."

"Thank you." As they lay there her hand made its way under his jacket. Initially it was just for warmth, and then it began to move over his stomach muscles. He grabbed her hand to stop it from moving back and forth on his chest

"Diane, I need you to stop that before I, at the very least, kiss you again."

"Maybe I'll kiss you this time."

She moved her mouth to his. The kiss started off tentative and sweet. He let her control the kiss at her pace until she let out a little moan and then he deepened the kiss. That caused her to moan again. He took the opportunity her parted lips offered and slipped his tongue into her mouth. She matched the movement. Heat exploded in her.

His hand moved down her back and cupped her jean clad bottom. Every nerve ending in her body came alive, craving more of his touch. She pressed her body closer to his. He kissed his way to her neck. She moaned his name. He stopped kissing her neck. He rested his face in the crook of her neck, inhaling her scent and trying to catch his breath. "Diane, we need to stop now or I won't be able to. I don't want to rush things."

If he hadn't stopped she wouldn't have been able to. She realized she hadn't wanted him to. This lack of control was foreign to her. The fog in her brain was clearing and she was embarrassed by the way she had behaved. Her body on the other hand wanted nothing more than for him to continue. Her heart was afraid it would be broken because she was falling hard for Jack.

"Jack, I don't understand my feelings."

"There's no need to understand. Let's just enjoy it." He knew if he let her think about her feelings too much she'd run from them and him. "We need to get you home. You have class tomorrow and I have an early morning. I know the proper etiquette is that I should take you home, but your car is ready and I thought you'd like to drive it. I can follow you to make sure you make it okay."

"How much do I owe you for the repair?"

"Nothing. It was an easy fix."

"You're a farmer, a musician, and a pseudo mechanic. What other talents do you have?"

"I'm a pretty good lover too."

Diane laughed nervously. From the way he kissed her she was sure he was. "Is there anything you can't do?"

"I can't walk on water," he smiled, "yet."

SOCIAL NETWORK

Diane Clark Status: This may be the most memorable Sunday I've ever had.

Comments:

Noli Freeman: More memorable than the Sunday we were in church for six hours next to the lady that smelled like garlic and had on the sequin hat?

Diane Clark: This Sunday was more memorable than that. Though, that Sunday was the only time I've ever seen Jesus depicted in sequins.

Jack Sloan Status: I didn't want this night to end.

chapter 6

AS USUAL, JACK SHOWED UP right on time Wednesday afternoon. Unfortunately, Diane was running behind because one of her professors had her come to her office to talk about a position at her firm after graduation. To get some experience straight out of college, even in a small college town, would be a great opportunity. The thought of being near Jack also crossed her mind. Jack's truck was already in the lot when Diane arrived at the apartment.

It had been two full days since she'd seen him last and she couldn't wait. She ran up the stairs excitedly. When she entered the apartment, her roommate, Megan, was cross examining Jack like he was on the witness stand. It's the type of scene usually reserved for fathers and their teenage daughter's first date.

"Sorry I'm late Jack. Hi Megan."

"You're worth the wait Di," he whispered into her ear as he took her into her arms for a hug.

"Hi" Megan said and exited the living room to her bedroom.

"It was nice to meet you," Jack said to Megan's retreating body. She waved over her shoulder and closed her door.

"Can you give me a few minutes?"

"Of course, but hurry. It's been two days and I've missed you."

She smiled and hurried to freshen up. It only took her a few minutes to change shirts and touch up her lipstick. As she was changing from her tennis shoes to her boots, Megan walked in. "Is this the guy you met over break?"

"He is." Diane smiled.

"Is he your type?"

"I don't know that I have a type. If I did, he'd fit."

"Really?"

"Really. He's different than he seems on the outside."

"Are you two serious?" her roommate asked concerned.

"We're just getting to know each other."

"Don't let him get in the way of your finals."

"I won't and he wouldn't. He knows how important school is to me."

"If he knew how important school was to you, he wouldn't be here to take you out when you have class tomorrow."

"Listen Megan, it's sweet of you to be concerned about me, but everything's fine."

"Fine," was Megan's final word as she left Diane's room.

"Your roommate is intense."

"She was more intense than usual. Finals have her on edge. What do you have planned for our second date?"

"Something fun as a break from the doldrums of studying."

After a very brief drive, Jack parked near a building Diane vaguely recognized. "Is this the Wonderlab?"

"It is."

"Isn't this place for elementary school kids?"

"It's for all ages. The website says so. I thought it would be fun for you to let your hair down and act like a kid again."

For the next hour they did act like kids again. They played in a bubble room and shot at each other with an air cannon. She couldn't remember how long it had been since she laughed so much that her stomach hurt. There was no longer any doubt in her mind that Jack was her type.

After their "play date" they went for pizza. Instead of sitting across from her in the booth, he sat next to her. She enjoyed the closeness.

"I'm nervous about meeting your parents."

"Don't be. If anything I should be nervous. My parents will likely drive you away with stories about me."

"Let's face it Jack, if the mullet didn't scare me off, stories of childhood pranks certainly won't." She added to herself that the only thing that came close to running her off was the confederate flag on the front of his truck the night they met. The thought turned her mood serious. "How will your parents react when they find out I'm black? Do you think they won't like me?"

"They didn't react to it one way or the other. I don't know if it mattered to them. Anyway, my father likes whatever my mother likes. The only things that could make my mother not like you is if you don't like her cooking or if you break her little boy's heart."

"They already know?"

"Momma asked how you looked so I told her. How did your parents react when you told them about me?"

"I haven't told them about you yet."

"Hmm," was his only response.

"It's not like you're a secret. I don't talk with my parents the way you talk with yours. My mother hasn't really talked to me much at all since Thanksgiving other than to make sure I was still alive. I did tell my best friend all about you."

"When do you think you'll tell your parents about us?"

"I was thinking around Christmas. It's best if I tell my mother things face to face. She's also still operating under the delusion that I'll get back with Dr. Insincere."

"Is that a possibility?"

She thought for a second how very deficient her ex-fiancée was in comparison to Jack. Jack was kinder, funnier, more thoughtful and sexier just to start. She didn't know if any man would ever be able to compare to the man she was getting to know. The thought made her smile.

"No, it's not possible."

Her pause made his chest feel a little tight. She'd been planning a life in a big city with a doctor and maybe a life in the country with a farmer wasn't as appealing. Perhaps she was just being nice and saying what she thought he wanted to hear.

"What about your family? Will me being white matter?"

"I can't see why it would. My mother won't approve of you because you're just Mr. Sloan and not Dr. Sloan. You could be a Minotaur, as long as you were Dr. Minotaur my mom wouldn't care."

"It sounds like you have a complicated relationship with your mother."

"It's not complicated at all. It's simple. She's in charge. She is the Empress of my life and if I don't live according to her dictates it's like I stabbed her in the back on the steps of the senate."

"Et tu Brute?"

She smiled that he got her Julius Caesar reference. "Exactly. I think she actually said that to me once."

"Did you ever just do what you wanted to?"

"Yes, all the time." She thought for a moment and then a smile crossed her face. "This one time, I went out for the high school basketball team. My mother thought sports, especially such a common sport, was improper for her children."

"Did you make the team?"

"Heck no. I'd never played and it showed. I was awful. I'm just grateful no one got video of it."

"I wish they did. I need proof that you're not perfect."

"Oh, I'm not perfect. Ask my mother. She'd tell you I'm not perfect." She rolled her eyes.

"Well I think you're perfect."

"Really?"

"Yes. I don't understand why your mom can't see that. Is she as hard on your brother?"

"Can we talk about something other than my mother? I have the rest of my life to discuss her with a therapist or four. What about your mom, where did she learn to cook?"

"She's from down south, Arkansas. Knowing how to make great food is a requirement there."

"How'd your parents meet?"

"They met at an FFA convention when they were in high school."

"FFA?" She shook her head not knowing the abbreviation.

"Future Farmers of America," he explained. "They say it was love at first sight. The story goes they wrote each other a letter every night and talked on the phone once a week. At the next convention, he greeted her by falling on one knee and proposing. She said yes, but there was another year of letters and phone calls because her parents wouldn't let her get married until she graduated high school. She got her diploma on Friday and was married on Saturday."

"That is the sweetest and most irrational thing I've ever heard."

"What's irrational about it?"

"They were young. They barely knew each other." She ticked each point off on a finger then threw her hands in the air. "How could they base the rest of their lives on two meetings? What about school? What about experiencing life before committing the rest of it to another person?"

"I was wondering where Nancy Grace was hiding." He smiled when she rolled her eyes at him. "They didn't want to live a life that didn't include the person they loved. They found a way to do everything they wanted to with each other. Momma got her degree and became a teacher and daddy took over the farm."

"But what if..."

"There are no what ifs Nancy Grace. They followed their hearts. They are living their happily ever after complete with a smart, handsome, and dang near perfect son."

"I didn't know you had a brother."

"Oh you're so funny. Let me get you back to your studying before your overprotective roommate tortures me for taking you away from your studying."

SOCIAL NETWORK

Jack Sloan's Status: It's important to follow your heart.

Diane Clark's Status: It's important to use your brain.

Comments:

Jack Sloan: Anytime you want to follow your heart, I'm the man for the job.

Diane Clark: I'll keep that in MIND.

chapter 7

JACK PULLED UP WITH DIANE on Sunday. No matter what he said, Diane remained nervous. She'd also brought a gift though he insisted it wasn't necessary. He helped her out of his truck in the traditional manner which consisted of a lot of body to body contact. He then kissed her on the forehead.

Before they could make it to the porch step, the door was opened. His mother came out onto the steps. She stood with her eyes narrowed and her hands on her hips as she looked at Diane from head to toe. Her perusal did not help ease Diane's nervousness.

"Well aren't you even more beautiful than Jack said."

"Thank you." Diane extended her hand towards the woman. "It's nice to meet you Mrs. Sloan."

Rose Sloan looked at her hand as if she had leprosy. Diane wished she had driven so she could flee back to the safety of her apartment. If his mother did not approve of her she was willing to cut her losses before her feelings developed any further.

"Get that hand nonsense out of here and give me a hug." She said stepping in with a bright smile that instantly relieved all of Diane's fears. Jack's mother kept her arm around Diane and guided her into the house. "We need to decide what you're going to call me. I'm either Rose or momma because I don't nearly have enough wrinkles to be Mrs. Sloan." Jack's mother pulled her closer and smiled brightly at her. "I'll show you a picture of my mother-in-law and you'll see."

"The way you cook, I'll call you whatever you tell me to."

"You're right she is a beautiful and smart one Jack."

Jack took her hand and gently pulled her away from his mother. "I'll return her to you in a moment. I want to give her a tour of the house."

"Take your time. I'll call you when dinner's ready."

Jack took Diane on a tour of the surprisingly large house. The last room they visited was his. She felt nervous being in his room alone with him with his parents in the house. His room was almost like a master suite. It had its own bathroom and a sitting area. He sat on the bed and she sat across from him in a chair.

"Did you really tell your mom I was beautiful and smart?"

"I just told her the truth."

"We have some time before dinner, why don't I play you a song."

"Are you going to play something original?"

"I thought I would."

As he began to play she saw that his love for music showed in his eyes. He was really talented. He played the guitar as if it were an extension of himself. Every strum of the strings made a beautiful sound that felt as though he were caressing her skin. His lyrics were beautiful in its simplicity and realness. His voice that heated her when he spoke made her erupt like a volcano when he sang. If this was him rusty she wondered what he sounded like polished.

Her silence when he finished playing made him nervous. She just sat there with her eyes closed. He was afraid he either put her to sleep or she hated it so much that she was afraid to even look at him.

"That was beautiful," she said finally. Her voice had the soft quality usually reserved for her first delicious bite of a baked good.

"Thank you," he said genuinely modest. He'd missed a note or two and if he were on American Idol they would have said he was a little pitchy.

"You're really good. Why haven't you played in a while?"

"Who am I going to play for? The pigs? Maybe the corn and soy."

"Play for you. It's obvious how happy you are when you play."

"What's the point? I don't want to chase an old dream. This farm is my dream now."

"Do you love music because it can make you money and bring you fame or do you love it because it satisfies your soul."

He didn't answer. She came to sit next to him on the bed and placed a reassuring hand on his arm. "What if you play for me? I'd love to be your audience."

He began to play another song. This one had no lyrics, but his fingers on the strings spoke to her. When he finished playing Diane initiated a kiss. Her hands cupped his face as she brought her lips to his. Like all her kisses, it started off hesitant and sweet. He let her control it for a while. It made him happy when she initiated the contact. It meant that he wasn't in this alone and she wanted him too. Her tongue touched his lips and he parted them instinctively. When her tongue touched his he took over control.

He moved his guitar from between them and pulled Diane closer so that her legs straddled his lap. His hands were on her back and he pulled her body into his. Her fingers were in his hair pulling his head into her. His hands slid down her body stopping to cup the firm roundness of her butt. He pulled it forward into him. She moaned and pulled forward into his rising desire. Her movement elicited a deep groan from him.

He kissed his way down her neck settling into her collar bone. Her body began to move on its own accord in search of more contact with him. His hands were on her waist gently guiding her back and forth against his hardening need. Her hands gripped his shoulders. She was afraid if she did not hold tight she'd float off the face of the earth. One of his hands moved back to cup her bottom while the other trailed a path up her torso, under her shirt until it reached the fullness of her breast. He gently squeezed its softness. His thumb traced circles around her hardened nipple.

"Oh Jack," she gasped in response to the feelings that were rushing through her body. She'd never felt this much desire. She'd never felt this close to anyone before.

He wanted her so much that he knew he had to stop. He wanted their first time to be more than a quickie before dinner. He wanted more for her than that. He stopped kissing her neck, but his face remained nestled there while he tried to catch his breath and corral his hormones. His hands weren't as quick to follow the order his brain had given to stop. His thumb continued to stimulate her nipple while his other had continued to keep her pressed against his erection. Slowly he mustered enough control to wrap his arms around her and pull her into a tight hug.

"I love you, Diane," he said softly into her ear.

She pushed back from him so that she could look him in the face. "You can't."

He smiled at her. "You can't deny me my feelings."

"We've only known each other for a short time. We can't have these feelings for each other."

His smile widened and his eyes sparkled. "You love me too," he stated.

"I-I did not say that."

"You said 'we' have these feelings. If you didn't mean love, what are your feelings for me?"

Her eyes began to water. "My feelings are, well, I feel. .." she was at a loss for words to describe how she felt other than love. "I do think I might possibly be falling in love with you, but it's not logical to feel that way this soon. I feel scared because I don't have any control of my feelings. Being out of control is scary. I'm afraid my heart's falling too fast and my head is going to have to clean up the mess when I get hurt."

"Di, I would never do anything to hurt you. I promise you that as fast as you're falling, I am falling faster and will be waiting to catch you when you land."

"You promise?" The question sounded the same way it would if a child were asking a parent for reassurance on the first day of school.

"I promise. But if you kiss me one more time I can't promise you that I'll be able to control myself enough to stop again."

She kissed him again. "What if I don't want you to stop?"

He gently slid her off of his lap. "Sweetheart I don't want our first time to be a quickie while my momma's cooking dinner downstairs."

That sobered her. "You're right. My first time should be more planned than this." She didn't realize she'd change the pronoun until it was too late.

"What do you mean your first time? Are you saying that you're a—"

"Virgin," she completed. "Yes, I am." She moved into him and nestled herself against his chest to avoid having to look him in the face during this conversation.

"But you were engaged and dating for four years. Are you saving yourself for marriage?"

"I wasn't, but it became that. He never brought the passion out of me. My relationship with him was always very logical and not very emotional. It made everyone else happy."

"Were you happy?"

"I was happy enough with him. I didn't really believe in love. It was a fictional concept to me until I saw a pair of blue eyes that made my heart start to act and feel independently of my head. Then I thought it was a possibility for me."

"Sounds like I won't have to wait four years for us to make love?"

"You're the one that stopped tonight, not me. The only thought that my body let my mind think was 'oh that feels so good'. I didn't even remember your mother is downstairs. My mother would roll over in her grave if she knew I was behaving so wantonly."

His expression grew serious. "I didn't think your mother was dead."

"She's not, but if she knew that I was behaving so wantonly she'd kill herself so that she could roll over in her grave."

There was a knock on the door that made her jump off the bed so quickly she almost broke the sound barrier.

He just smiled at her over reaction. His mother's voice floated through the door telling them dinner was ready.

If it was possible, Diane thought that dinner fresh off the stove was even better than the leftovers she'd been warming in the microwave. Over the course of dinner she saw where Jack got his character from.

By the end of the meal Diane was instructed to call Jack's parents momma and dad because that's what everyone calls them. The word momma seemed strange coming off her lips since she'd not used it since she was in pre-K and her mother told her she preferred to be called mother.

Dinner that night was how she always imagined family dinners should be. It was so foreign from her family's meals. Her family meals felt more like a staff meeting with talk of goals and strategy. There was rarely any laughter and the food was barely edible.

Diane was re-evaluating her life goals. Power suits and corner offices with windows no longer held the same appeal as they did before her car broke down. There was now a longing for family dinners and kisses from the man she loved in its place.

DRIVING OUT TO THE farm for dinner each night became a nightly ritual for Diane. The food was far better than the normal college fare. Each evening after dinner, they would go out to the empty field to spend some time alone together. They would lay under the stars. Jack liked it because the cold December nights forced Diane to move close to him. She would never say, but that was her favorite part too. She also liked how time seemed to stand still and left them in a world of their own.

There were also the kisses. He'd kiss her to within an inch of her life each time they came out. She did not know kisses could feel the way his did. She'd only ever kissed two men. There was her high school boyfriend that had no clue what he was doing so he couldn't make it enjoyable for her. Then there was Alan that was too self-centered to care if it was enjoyable for her. Jack would always stop just before she was about to lose total control.

There was no doubt in her mind that she was full-fledged in love with Jack. It still scared her too much to say the words. When he confessed his love for her, she'd just say "me too" which seemed just fine with him.

SOCIAL NETWORK

Diane Clark's status: I'm starting to re-prioritize my goals.

Comments:

Ryan Clark: Did you get approval from our mother before you made the decision to decide something for yourself?

Diane Clark's relationship status changed to in a relationship.

Jack Sloan, Amara Adams and 7 others like this.

Jack Sloan's relationship status changed to in a relationship.

Diane Clark, Cooper Smith and 12 others like this.

Message from Ryan Clark to Diane Clark: Who is Jack Sloan? What kind of relationship are you in with him?

Message from Diane Clark to Ryan Clark: It's too much to explain in a message. I'll call you.

chapter 8

"**Y**OU SPENT THE NIGHT WITH that Jack guy?" Megan greeted Diane in a less than welcoming manner as she came through the door early one morning.

"Hello to you too," Diane said, taken aback by her roommate's tone. Megan seemed different from her normally cheery self lately and she didn't know why. "Yes, I stayed at Jack's last night."

"You guys have barely known each other for a month and you're sleeping with him?"

Though Diane felt no need to explain to her roommate, she did. "We're not sleeping together. I slept at the farm last night because I was too tired to drive back. I slept in the guest room if you must know."

"It seems like you and Jack are getting pretty serious. I saw you changed your relationship status last night."

"Yeah, I guess we are pretty serious." Despite her displeasure with the conversation, Diane could not help but smile when she thought of him.

"So he's not just someone to help you get over Alan?"

"No he's not. I've never thought of him that way."

"So you see a future with him?"

"I don't know, maybe. We might last through tomorrow or until we're 90. I don't know, my crystal ball is broken." Sarcasm was Diane's defense mechanism and she was feeling defensive about Megan's tone and line of questions.

"Do you think he sees a future with you?"

"I can't predict the future anymore. My crystal ball is in the shop after I tried to predict when the Kardashian's fifteen minutes of fame would be up. Do you have a problem with Jack?"

"No, I barely know Jack. But you barely know him either."

"Is that what the problem is Megan?" Diane couldn't understand why her roommate was suddenly so protective of her all of a sudden. They weren't really friends. They were just roommates. The only reason they were even that was because they both wanted to move out of student housing at the same time a couple of years ago.

"The problem is that you shouldn't be thinking of dating him."

"Why not?"

"Maybe you haven't noticed but you two aren't on the same level."

"Do you think I'm too good for him because he didn't go to college?"

"I don't think you're too good for him. I think he's too good for someone like you."

"You just said you barely know him so how is it that he's too good for me?" Diane was beyond frustrated with this conversation and really just wanted to shower and change for class.

"Come on Diane, I know you're not stupid. Do you really need me to spell it out Diane?"

"Yes I do because I know that what I'm thinking you're saying can't be what you're saying because it's not 1952."

"If you think what I'm saying is that he shouldn't be dating you because you're black then you're right on the money."

Diane looked at her like she was crazy. "I can't believe you're saying this white supremacist mess. We've known each other since freshman year. How could you be friends and roommates with someone that's inferior?"

"I don't think you're inferior Diane. And I am not a supremacist. I believe you all should have equal rights and opportunities. I just don't believe God intended us to mix. No little half breed babies are going to come from a friendship."

"Don't bring God into this because Jesus is crying at the words coming out of your mouth," Diane said pointing her finger at Megan.

"If He's crying over anything it's over you and Jack. God says in the Bible that the different races shouldn't be together."

"Really? Is that in the racist propaganda translation of the Bible? In Galatians it clearly states that there is no race and we are all one in Christ."

"It also says that a marriage should not be between two people that are unequally yoked."

"If that's the case you should have been objecting to me and Alan because the inequality of the yolks is referring to believers and nonbelievers." Diane was so upset she actually said the name which she'd vowed never to say again.

"Do you think you're more than just some curiosity to him? He just only wants to see what it's like to screw a black girl. Do you think he'll still be around once he gets what's in your panties?" With each question and accusation Megan moved closer to Diane. Diane held her ground, refusing to back away.

"Well that means he'll be around for a long time. I'm not easy like you. The only thing drops faster than your panties is you to your knees with your mouth open."

Megan gasped, insulted by the truth. "Maybe if it did you'd still have a fiancée. And if you think he's been celibate the past few years waiting to for you then you should ask Porsche, Mercedes, and all your other little ghetto friends named after cars their parents couldn't afford."

Diane took a deep breath to calm the urge to hit her roommate because she knew she'd lose that fight. Megan had been in enough drunken girls gone wild fights in bars to earn a title belt. "I don't have time for this. I need to get ready for class. I hope there won't be a cross burning outside my bedroom door when I come out." Diane slammed the door behind her and locked it.

"HEY, DIANE."

"Hi, Andre. How are you?"

"I'm good. What's up with you though?"

"Megan and I had an argument."

"What ya get into it 'bout?"

Diane was always taken aback when it was just her and Andre speaking alone because his dialect was totally different. In class and amongst any multi-racial group he spoke full words without any slang vernacular, but that was different when only blacks were present.

"Megan doesn't like the guy I'm dating."

"What up wit' him?"

"Nothing's wrong with him." That smile appeared again as it normally did when she thought about Jack. "Megan's the one that has the problem. She came out of the closet."

"Naw! She been wit' too many guys for me to believe that."

Diane realized the misunderstanding. "Oh, not that closet. She came out of the racist closet. She's one of those closeted, covert racist. She doesn't think I should be dating Jack because he's white."

"Yo' new dude is white?"

"He is."

"Megan not the one in the closet. Her reasoning is racist, but she right. Why a smart sista like you go from a good black man to Mr. Charlie?"

Diane was dumbfounded. She couldn't believe this was happening again. Apparently the closet of racists was packed tight with fools. Unfortunately, he didn't need her to contribute to this conversation.

"You're too smart to fall for the lies from the descendants of the men who raped and murdered your ancestors. Do you think his white parents taught him how to love, respect and protect a black women the way a black man was raised to?"

"Those are the qualities that any man should have, regardless of race. Andre, I think you're as racist as Megan," she said exacerbated.

"A black man can't be racist."

"If you choose to believe that, I won't try to talk you off that ledge. My father taught me that arguing with a fool makes me one too." Diane turned to walk away, but Andre grabbed her arm. She snatched it back and walked away with long, quick strides before he could get anymore hate out.

WHEN DIANE GOT BACK to the apartment Megan wasn't there as usual on Thursday. She did not think she could handle another confrontation, plus she did not feel comfortable there anymore. She packed a few clothes and her books then called Jack.

"Hello Nancy Grace. How's your day?"

"Not good. Can I stay out at the farm this weekend?"

"Of course you can. What's wrong Di?"

"I'll explain why when I get there."

When she arrived at Jack's a half hour later his mother answered the door and greeted her with a hug.

"Jack said you didn't have a good day and you look about ready to skin a cat. What happened? Do I need to go get my gun?"

Diane chuckled. She was touched by the genuine concern in the other woman's voice. Diane let tears of exasperation and weariness fall from her face.

"No guns are necessary. The place to stay is more than enough. Just let me take my bags to the room."

"Nonsense. You leave that bag be and let that boy of mine carry it. You come have a seat and tell me what's got you so bothered while I finish dinner."

"You need help with dinner."

"I never need help with cooking, but your help will get it done faster," Rose said with a wink.

Rose gave a quick demonstration on how to mash the potatoes. Diane was shocked when almost two sticks of butter (never margarine) and whole milk were added to the bowl of potatoes. She knew when she tasted them before that they were not diet food, but she did not know she should schedule an echo cardiogram after eating them. Her mother's mashed potatoes were straight from the box and not quite so flavorful, now she knew why.

"Talk child. Tell me what's wrong."

"My roommate doesn't like Jack and me dating."

"Does she like that doctor better? Did the boy part the Red Sea or something?"

"No, but your son thinks he's pretty close to walking on water."

"I am sure he does, but that would make me the Virgin Mary. My Pete can testify to the fact that this rose's bud was picked a long time ago."

"Momma!" "Rose!" Jack and his father said simultaneously.

"What?"

"Everybody doesn't need to know our business," Pete said.

"And I just don't want to hear that stuff." Jack added.

"It's not like I was talking about what we did last night. I am just stating the fact that I am no virgin." Pete kissed Rose on her cheek and wrapped his arms around her waist. He whispered something in her ear that did the impossible and made her blush.

Jack stooped down in front of Diane and looked into her eyes as if he could discern exactly what was wrong without any words. He did not know what was wrong, but he knew what to say to make it better.

"I love you," he said softly.

Diane smiled and kissed him in response. She still wasn't ready to say those words because they scared her.

"Let me go clean up and we can go for a walk so you can tell me what's wrong."

"You go clean up and but she'll be talking right here about what's wrong. I want to hear it too."

"They could be clear across town and you'd hear what she said. You hear like a hawk." Pete said.

"It is eyes like a hawk and ears like a bat," Momma corrected.

Jack picked up Diane's bag and headed upstairs.

"She's batty alright," Pete said to Jack as he followed him up the stairs.

"I heard that," Rose called after them.

"I'm sure you did." Pete said chuckling.

"WHERE'S YOUR FATHER?" Rose asked a half hour later when Jack returned alone.

"He's lying down until dinner."

"How was he today?" she asked concerned.

"He was good, slower than normal, but good."

"I wish he would just let you run the show."

"Momma, he's afraid if he stops doing, he'll stop being."

"I swear this boy's been smarter since he's known you Diane."

"Smart isn't contagious Momma."

"Maybe stupid is because I can't think of too many reasons she's with the likes of you," she said jokingly.

"It's your cooking Momma. He said I couldn't have any more if I wasn't with him."

"Ladies, the love in the room is overwhelming." Jack said sitting in the chair next to Diane. He'd changed from his work jeans and flannel to his good jeans and flannel. The difference between the two was the amount of wear and tear. He wore both well. Diane never thought she'd find snug fitting jeans sexy.

"I've waited long enough, what's going on with your roommate Diane?" Rose said turning her attention to the couple at the table.

"She doesn't think Jack and I should be dating."

Jack took her hands into his. "What she thinks doesn't matter."

"It's not just her. A classmate of mine had his own separate but equally stupid reasons for thinking we shouldn't be together."

"What anybody besides you and me thinks doesn't matter. You know that right?"

She wanted to believe it, but shouldn't couldn't. "She came from so far out of left field."

Jack's hands tightened around hers. "What are their reasons?"

"Because they're stupid and racist. She doesn't like that I'm black and he didn't like that you're white. She was so aggressive about it that I don't feel safe in that apartment."

His eyes darkened and his jaw clenched. "Did she touch you?"

"No. The words got pretty intense but it didn't escalate into a physical confrontation."

"You didn't pack enough bags to stay for long," Rose said.

"Are you that afraid of her?" Jack asked.

"I honestly don't know if I should be or not. She didn't threaten me or anything, but I saw a totally different person today, so I'm not certain of what she's capable of."

"I don't want you living with her anymore." It was Rose who said this with a hint of venom in her voice.

"It'll be hard to find a place I can afford since I've already paid through the semester."

"Can you afford free? Because you're staying here," Rose said unwaveringly.

"I can't ask you to let me stay here."

"You're not asking, we're offering." Jack said. "I'm with Momma. You can't stay there."

"I know I can't, but I don't want to put you out. You all have enough going on, you don't need to worry about me."

"You're not putting us out. I'd be more worried about you if you weren't here."

His smile showed more than concern. "Just concern? No ulterior motives Jack?"

"It's 90% concern and 8% being able to see you every day."

"What about the other 2%?" He just smiled that crooked little smile that showed his dimple best.

"So tell us what your roommate said?" Rose said not wanting to see her son make out with Diane in her kitchen.

Diane retold the exchange she had with Megan. Though she was hesitant about telling the part about her being only a curiosity to Jack, but she said it in the end. She even told them about how easy she said Megan was and her run in with Andre after class.

"I'm glad you didn't just let her say that malarkey without getting in a couple of good ones yourself. Jack, go get your dad. Diane, you can set the table." Rose gave the instructions, easily integrating Diane even more into the family dinner routine.

They all sat around the table and ate dinner together, the conversation drifted away from the dramatic events of the day to their normal chatter. Everyone had their take on the situation. They laughed and talked and ate. Once again she was thinking how much different it was from her family dinners. One difference was there were no waiters or waitresses, the main difference though was the ease with which everyone interacted. The only expectation they had of each other was the expectation of happiness.

After dinner Diane helped Jack clean up the kitchen then he drove her out to "their spot". They lay in the bed of his truck under a blanket, looking up at the stars, being in Jack's arms made her forget the stress of the day.

"Jack, Megan and Andre are not the only ones that feel that way," she said breaking the silence.

"I know, but it only matters what we think."

"I wish that were true, but we don't live in a cocoon separated from everyone else. Is love enough to battle the stupidity of the world?"

He sat up on his elbow and looked down at her. "For every one intolerant Megan in this world is five people that support us and another four people that don't give a flying care. I can't tell you how hard or easy it'll be for us or that we won't have folks trying to tear us apart just because of our differences in skin color. What I can tell you though, is that life is too short to live with the regret of not giving love and happiness a chance."

"Jack I'm afraid. I'm afraid of the difficulties. I'm most afraid I'll lose being in the arms of the man I love looking up at the stars with a belly full of his momma's cooking."

"The man you love?"

As the realization sunk in that she'd finally said she loved him, his mouth covered her lips. She gave into her heart and let go of any thought other than the sensation of kissing his unshaven upper lip. It was rough and erotic against her skin as he kissed his way down her neck.

SOCIAL NETWORK

Diane Clark's status: What a day?! It's unfortunate that people never cease to surprise me with their stupidity.

Jack Sloan's status: I'll never get tired of hearing her say those words.

Comments:

Diane Clark: You'll never get tired of your mother saying dinner's ready.

chapter 9

DIANE WAS SHOCKED TO SEE her parents in her apartment when she opened the door early Sunday afternoon. Several emotions spun through her at once, but dread is what the wheel stopped on.

"Mother, Daddy what are you doing here?" She did not know if it was out of shock or embarrassment that kept her from walking through the door and revealing Jack as well. It wasn't shock, or embarrassment, it was protection that she felt. She wanted to protect her relationship from her Mother.

"Diane! We've been worried sick," her father said, looking suddenly relieved.

"Why?" Diane said giving her father a hug and a warm smile. "Hi, Daddy."

"Your phone is dead," her mother said with an emotionless tone.

"Yes it is," Diane said reinforcing the statement unnecessarily. "I left my charger here. Our normal call is on Sunday so why are you alarmed that you drove all the way down here?"

"When I could not reach you on your cell Thursday or Friday, I called the apartment. Your roommate said you had moved out. When there was still no word from you we thought maybe your roommate was not joking when she said you had moved in with some boy you just met. "

Jack gently pushed the door all the way open which prompted Diane to step forward. "I would be the boy she just met ma'am. Jack Sloan."

He extended his hand but Diane's mother ignored it as though it was at best irrelevant or at worse contaminated with a drug resistant plague.

Diane's father came forward and firmly took Jack's hand into his. "I'm Robert Clark, Diane's father. This is her mother Catherine."

"Diane, what exactly is going on here?" Catherine moved the conversation forward, seeing no need for pleasant introductions.

"Mother, this is Jack. Since Thanksgiving we have been..." Diane paused looking for the best word to describe her relationship with Jack.

"Dating," Jack provided. This was a different side of Diane. She was unsure of herself.

"Thank you, Jack," she said softly with an easy smile that contradicted the panic in her eyes.

"Diane, how are you dating when you are engaged?"

"Mother, I'm not engaged."

"Fine. You were engaged on Wednesday then dating on Thursday? Or were you dating before you abruptly called off the engagement? If so, I did not raise you like that."

Diane did not respond. It seemed that she was willing herself to stay where she was and not flee out of the door. Jack put a comforting hand of support on Diane's mid back.

"Ma'am, your daughter and I met when I stopped to help her after her car broke down the day before Thanksgiving."

"Jack is it?" Catherine said his name as though it was a bitter tea that had been steeped too long. "I am speaking to my daughter. If you would be so kind as to remove your hand from my daughter it would be appreciated."

Jack wasn't quite certain why he felt the need to protect Diane from her own mother, but he did. Diane did not seem like the beautiful flower she normally was, but one that had been withered by harsh sunlight. Instead of removing his hand, he began to rub her back with his thumb. He was about to respond when Robert shot him a sympathetic look and a slight shake of his head to deter him from responding.

"Sweetie, why don't we all sit and you can tell us what's going on," Diane's father said trying to bring the boiling tension to a simmer.

Catherine sat first and motioned for her daughter to sit next to her. Hesitantly Diane took the seat next to her mother. Robert sat in the only remaining chair next to the end of the couch nearest Catherine and Jack sat on the arm of the couch next to Diane.

"When did your car break down?" Robert asked Diane.

"It broke down on the way home just before Thanksgiving."

"Why didn't you call for help?" her father asked

"My phone had died after talking to Mother and Dr. Insincere...Alan for almost two and a half hours straight."

"Are you saying this is somehow my fault?" Catherine said with her arms crossed and the same disapproving look on her face that she'd had since Jack and Diane had arrived.

"I'm not saying that at all." Diane said holding back the exasperation she felt from being heard in her voice. "I am simply answering Daddy's question."

"After sitting on the side of the road with no one else in sight for about an hour, Jack pulled up and helped."

"Why didn't you tell me your car needed to be repaired? I could have had it fixed by now."

"I fixed it, Sir. She had it back by the following Sunday."

"You are a mechanic?" Catherine asked saying the word mechanic as if it were a synonym for hooligan.

"No ma'am. I'm a farmer." Jack was finding it difficult to maintain the polite tone like his momma raised him. He did not want to make an enemy out of Diane's mother even if every word coming out of her mouth sounded like they were coming from the mythological banshee.

"Oh good Lord," Catherine mumbled.

"Sweetie, what did your roommate mean when she said you'd moved in with Jack?" Robert said getting the conversation back on course.

"I haven't moved in with Jack, yet. I stayed the last couple of nights at his house."

"Oh, good Lord in heaven," Catherine said.

"What do you mean by yet?" Robert asked and for the first time turned a less than amicable eye to Jack.

"Just to clarify sir, she didn't stay with me. She had her own room at my parent's house out on the farm. Did her roommate also tell you that she'd made some racist comments that caused Di not to feel safe sleeping in the apartment?"

"Her name is Diane, not Di," Catherine said.

Jack just stared at her. He could not seriously believe that what stood out in that question was his use of a shortened form of Diane's name. He also found it rather sad that neither Robert nor Diane seemed to be phased by this.

"What racist comments?" Robert asked to stay the course of the conversation.

"Thursday morning when I came back from Jack's..."

"Excuse me?" her father interrupted.

"She'd come out to the farm for dinner with me and my family and fell asleep while studying afterwards," Jack said. "Once again, she had her own room Sir."

"He didn't think it was safe for me to drive back sleepy," Diane continued. "So, his Momma offered me one of their spare rooms," she finished.

"Oh, good Lord in heaven, have mercy on me," Catherine said in response to her daughter's use of the word Momma.

"When I returned home the next morning, Megan expressed her disapproval of me dating someone that was white because being black makes me inferior."

"If she threatened you with any harm we need to call the police."

"She didn't threaten me, but the conversation got pretty heated and I just didn't feel safe. I didn't know what she was capable of because it was a whole different Megan."

"You should have called us instead of running to people you barely know. We are your parents," Catherine said.

"I didn't want to worry you Mother." Diane felt the statement was true enough to not be a lie. The first person she thought of calling was Jack. Contacting her parents was an afterthought.

"I think leaving was the best thing to do Sweetie, but your Mother is right. You should have called us to let us know what was going on."

Diane looked nervously at Jack. "Since I hadn't told you about Jack, I felt that was too much to explain over the phone. I planned on telling you everything when I came home for Christmas next weekend."

Jack had assumed from her parents' earlier statements that Diane hadn't told them about him. Her confirmation of that fact had him unsettled. He wasn't sure how he felt about being her secret.

"Were you returning because you and Megan straightened things out?" her father asked.

"No, Daddy. I haven't spoken to her since Thursday. I don't know what there is to straighten out. She believes that blacks are okay as long as they know their place and apparently I am out of my place. Jack's family has offered me a room at the farm and I've accepted."

"That may be best since there's only a week left before finals," Robert agreed shocking everyone.

"You cannot possibly be serious." Catherine cut her husband a look that would kill if he'd not built up an immunity to it over the years.

"We can find an apartment for next semester over winter break."

"Daddy, I checked and the lease can't be broken without paying a steep penalty. If I moved into another place you'd practically be paying rent at two places and that seems excessive."

"We offered for her to stay out at the farm. We have plenty of room."

"Give me strength," Catherine said to no one in particular or perhaps it was a prayer to God.

"Well. There seems to be some logic to that," Robert said. He looked from Jack to his daughter and then back to Jack. "Can we come out to your farm and meet your parents? I'd like to see where my daughter may be staying."

"Yes sir. Just let me call and let them know we'll have two more for supper."

Catherine mumbled something with the only intelligible words being Jesus, supper and Mayberry.

It took Diane only a few minutes to pack and grab her phone charger. Once outside Diane started towards the safety of Jack's truck to head to the farm.

"Diane, where are you going?" her mother chastised her. "You are riding with us."

"Mother, it would be rude to have Jack ride by himself."

"You are right. Your father can ride with him." Catherine didn't wait for any further discussion of the matter.

Jack stood closely behind Diane and whispered in her ear, "I'll drive fast to make the ride quick." He kissed her on the top of her head and headed to his truck. She smiled. He knew her so well it was like he was reading her mind. She felt herself fall a little more in love.

The door to the car had barely closed before her mother began her inquisition. "Diane, is this Jack Sloan boy just to help you get over Alan?"

drive with her mother. Jack walked over to Diane and took her by the hand then kissed her on the head.

"You ok?" he asked deeply in her ear.

She was now. She liked that he was concerned about her. It was also attractive that he felt the need to protect her, even from her own mother. She smiled up at him and nodded then rose on her tiptoe to brush a quick kiss on his lips.

Her mother cleared her throat and said, "It is rather cold out here, perhaps we should go in."

As they walked through the front door, Jack's Momma came from the kitchen smiling and drying her hands on a dish towel hanging from the waistband of her apron. She kissed Diane on her cheek as usual. She then approached Catherine with a smile.

"You must be Cathy," she said and forced the other woman into a hug. "Di is the spittin' image of you."

"It is Catherine and my daughter's name is Diane," she said, not returning the unwelcomed embrace.

"Isn't that what I said?" Before Catherine could respond she'd moved over towards Robert. "You must be Rob." She surprised him with a warm friendly hug as well. "You're not lacking in the looks department either."

"It is Robert," Catherine corrected.

"Isn't that what I said?"

"Mrs. Clark, Robert, this is my mother Rose Sloan."

"Jack, take their coats and put them in the closet please. Rob, my husband is in the family room watching football if you and Jack want to join him. Di, I know you want to join them too, but I'd like your help in the kitchen for a bit. Cathy, Jack will introduce you to my husband and then you can join us girls in the kitchen."

"It is Catherine," she said not hiding the frustration by the use of the shortened form of her name.

"Isn't that what I said?" Rose said feigning ignorance with a glint of amusement in her eye.

Everyone followed Roses' instructions, even Catherine, though with a slight delay in protest. She was used to doing the ordering around and not being ordered around.

"Rose, why do you keep calling my mother Cathy?"

"Because it is really getting her goat. It's really funny that something so small would bother her so."

"All this time I thought you were so sweet."

"Too much sweetness causes cavities."

"DAD, THIS IS CATHERINE and Robert Clark, Diane's parents. Mr. and Mrs. Clark this is my father Peter Sloan."

Jack was glad to see that his dad hadn't tried to stand. Last time he tried to stand too quickly he'd gotten dizzy and lost his balance. He stretched his hand out. Catherine looked a might perturbed that Peter had failed to rise to greet her and she kept her arms folded in front of her. When Peter tried to stand to appease her, Jack waved him off.

Robert took a step forward and shook Peter's hand. "Nice to meet you. You can call me Robert."

"Nice to meet you too. Call me Pete. Please have a seat." Robert sat in the recliner next to Pete.

"Jack, can you direct me to the restroom?"

"What kind of car do you drive Robert?"

Jack heard the question as he left the room. He knew this was the question his father asked to judge every man's character. Degrees and net worth meant nothing to Peter if you did not drive American.

"A three year old Charger. I want the new Camaro, but I'm having a hard time getting that one by my wife."

Jack was relieved. Not only did he drive American, but he'd mentioned wanting a Chevy product.

"Chevy makes a mighty fine vehicle. I've had my truck for fifteen years and in runs like I bought it tomorrow." Pete laughed at his own joke. "You can't go wrong with anything made in Detroit. If Diane wasn't driving one of them foreign jobs she wouldn't have broken down on the side of the road."

"I'm thankful for that foreign car. If she were driving American, I wouldn't have met her that day," Jack said from the doorway of the room. He was waiting for Catherine so he could escort her to the kitchen.

DIANE SAT AT THE table cutting cucumber and tomatoes for the salad while Rose stood at the stove frying pork chops in a cast iron skillet. This had become their routine, talking and laughing while fixing dinner. They were both laughing about one of Jack's childhood stories when Jack escorted Catherine into the large kitchen.

"Jack, Momma just told me another story about you. Pretty soon I'll have the whole scoop on you."

Catherine felt disconcerted by her daughter's use of the affectionate term for this other woman. She was also taken aback by the easy camaraderie the two shared. Her relationship with her daughter was full of tension with an origin unknown to Catherine. The relationship between Diane and Rose was what Catherine had always wanted with her daughter, but had never been able to obtain. Her daughter's closeness to her father was one thing, but this hurt more.

To knock that point home, Diane stood. "I've finished the salad. May I go watch the game now?"

It seemed to Catherine that Diane could not get away from her fast enough and that her daughter interacted with Rose as if she were her mother. Catherine realized that she felt jealous that her daughter was giving motherly affection to a woman she hadn't known existed until today. She wondered if her daughter would keep a secret from Rose the way she'd kept her relationship with Jack secret from her.

"Thank you for offering my daughter a place to stay for the remainder of the semester."

"It was no problem. When she told us what her roommate said, we didn't feel she'd be safe there."

Diane had called them before her own family. The pain fed by the closeness with these relative strangers grew in Catherine. "Yes, I agree. It is probably best she not stay there. She does not need any distractions during finals. After the break we can find someplace else for her to stay."

Rose just smiled but did not respond and the room went quiet for a few awkward moments. Finally Catherine broke the silence. "We must compensate you for her expenses."

"No need. She's been eating here regularly for the last few weeks and it just means a few less leftovers for my midnight snack. She has been going through desserts though. She has quite the sweet tooth."

The room fell silent once again as Catherine contemplated how well Rose knew her daughter and how much Jack seemed to care for Diane. It had not passed her notice that he had even tried to protect Diane from her.

"Is there anything I can do to help?" Catherine asked.

"Oh no, you're a guest."

Diane was a guest, but she was not treated as such. "You have a lovely home," she said changing the subject before it fell into more silence.

"Thank you. I'll give you a tour of the house after supper. If it weren't so cold, I'd take you on the full tour of the farm."

At dinner Diane sat between her mother and Jack's mother. Jack was across the table giving her indecent smiles. The smiles weren't really indecent, but they made her have indecent thoughts.

"These pork chops are better than the ones my mother used to make," Robert said as he cut off another bite.

"It's the freshness," Jack's father responded. "We have a place where we can get them really fresh." Once again he was the only one to laugh at his lame humor.

"I'd love to take some home. Where do you get them from?" Robert asked

"They raise pigs, I mean hogs, Daddy," Diane answered her father's question.

"Sweetie, can you use your phone to reserve us a room in town. I think it's best we wait until the morning to head back home."

"Nonsense, you can stay here. We have plenty of room," Rose said.

"That is a kind offer, but a hotel will be just fine," Catherine said wanting to be alone with her husband to process the events of the day.

"We insist. There's no need for you to spend your money on a room," Jack's father said.

"We have the money so it is not a problem for us to get a room," Catherine said defensively.

"It won't be a problem to stay here either Catherine," Robert simply stated to his wife.

THE REST OF DINNER passed with only a few stilted words. Late that night Jack found a moment of time alone with Robert.

"May I speak with you a moment sir?"

"Yes Jack."

They walked into the den and sat in two chairs that are separated by a small table with a lamp on it. Jack took a deep breath and began to speak.

"Sir, I know you didn't even know of my existence prior to this afternoon. I also know that I've only known your daughter for a brief amount of time. That being said, I want you to know that I have thought greatly about this. What I'm getting at sir is that I would like your permission to ask your daughter to marry me?"

Robert did not say anything for a moment. Jack looked at the desk across the room instead of at the other man. His hands rested clasped together on his lap so that he wouldn't fidget with them nervously.

"You definitely have not known her long. Are you certain?"

"Sir, I've never been more certain of anything in my life."

"Is she pregnant?"

"No sir. I respect that she wants to wait until she's married."

"Is that the reason then?"

Uncomfortable with discussing sex with Diane's father, Jack smiled an awkward smile. "Not at all, I just love your daughter sir."

"If you truly love her now, you'll love her a year from now. Why the rush?"

"I've come to understand how fragile life can be and not to waste a single moment. I don't want to squander time when I know this is what I want."

"This may be what you want, but what about what Diane wants."

"I think she feels the same about me. She is cautious because it isn't logical to her. I suspect I'll have to ask her about three times before she says yes."

Robert chuckled because he knew his daughter could be overly cautious. "If I say no will you hold off from asking her?"

"With all due respect sir, I likely will still ask her."

Robert smiled. He liked that Jack was respectful, honest and did not back down from his feelings. "Are you trying to have a quick wedding?"

"Whatever Di wants. The next day or the next year is fine as long as she becomes my wife."

"It's good you know before marriage who is in charge. That being said, the wedding will likely be based on what Catherine wants. Even if she's not thrilled about you two getting married, which she likely won't be, there's no way she won't have something to do with the planning."

"If that's what Di wants, that's fine." Jack simply stated expressing that this was about what Diane wanted and not her mother.

"I know it's old fashion for you to ask for her hand, but I appreciate that you did. Alan didn't bother to. If he had I don't know that I would have said yes. I never trusted that boy, he has shifty eyes. Catherine and I had only been dating for a couple of weeks before we married. Granted we'd known each other longer than you and Diane. I can understand that when you know, you know, even if you can't explain how or why."

"Does that mean I have your blessing sir?" Jack asked for clarification.

"It does. Though I think it may be best for me not to mention this conversation to my wife."

"I can handle that."

SOCIAL NETWORK

Message Diane Clark to Ryan Clark: Thanks for the warning about Mom and Dad.

Message Ryan Clark to Diane Clark: You're welcome. I did try to warn you, but your phone's dead.

Message Diane Clark to Ryan Clark: You could have sent me a message, an email, or used smoked signals. You know I hate being caught off guard.

Message Ryan Clark to Diane Clark: I'm sorry I
could have been more persistent, but I have a few
things in my own life that I'm trying to deal with.

Jack Sloan's status: Keep your phones charged. If
you don't it may result in a surprise visit from
your girlfriend's parents.

chapter 10

DIANE STEPPED OUT OF HER final exam confident that she had passed it. She reached into her purse for her phone to call Jack. He'd sent a text just before her exam that said he needed her with a wink.

"Hey Di," he said wearily.

"What's wrong? It sounds like you're crying."

There was a pause before he spoke so softly the words were almost inaudible. "I need you."

"I'll be at the farm in twenty minutes."

"I'm not at the farm. I'm at the hospital in town."

Diane stopped in her tracks. "What's happened?"

"Dad passed out. Di, I know you have finals, but I could sure use to see you right now."

"Don't worry about my finals. I'll be there."

Jack hugged Diane so tightly when he saw her that it felt like she became part of him. When he let go she kissed him comfortingly.

"Thank you for coming." He took her hand in his.

"No need to thank me for being where I'm supposed to be. What happened? How serious is it?"

Jack explained, "Back in October there was a spot on a CAT Scan Dad had. It was small and Dad convinced the doctors to wait until after the holidays to do a biopsy. Then today, I found him passed out in the barn." Tears began to fall from Jack's blue eyes.

"Oh, Jack." She wiped the tears away.

"He was still breathing and had a pulse but he wouldn't respond. I was so scared. I didn't know what to do." Diane began to cry too. She began to stroke the back of his hand with her thumb. "They did another scan and it showed a larger spot. It was more aggressive than they thought. They went in for emergency surgery because they didn't want to chance it getting any bigger."

Diane wrapped her arms around him and laid her head on his chest. It was as much to comfort him as it was to comfort herself.

"Where's Momma?" Diane asked.

"She's lying down in the family hospitality room."

"I want to go check on her," she said

"I'll come with you."

They walked to the room and his mother was sleeping. The stress of the day prompted her to take a nap at the time she normally would have been adding a half a pound of butter to something for dinner. Jack returned to their waiting room. Diane went and got them something to eat from the cafeteria. They sat for a couple of hours, exchanging few words.

"You should have called me sooner?"

"I didn't want to throw you off from taking your exam."

Diane was amazed that he could think of her when his world was rocked.

"I'll be right back. Let me go check on Momma again," Diane said

Jack smiled internally at the love and concern she showed for him and his parents. "I love you, Diane."

"I love you too, Jack."

Diane walked into the room where Rose was sleeping. Diane did not want to disturb her so she pulled the covers up to keep the chill off.

"Boy, I told you to stop fussing over me."

"It's not Jack. It's me, Diane."

"Oh, hi sweetheart, I'm so glad you're here. Jack's beside himself. You can help keep him calm and convince him to go home."

"I don't think he's going home anytime soon."

"You convince him to. He can't do surgery and he doesn't know how to do lab work so the best thing he can do for me and his dad right now is rest."

"Is there something I can get you before I go?"

"No I'm fine. I'm so glad Jack has you. Last time he didn't cope too well with his father being in the hospital. I know I don't have to worry about him because you'll be there for him this time."

"I'm here for you too."

"I know sweetheart. What you can do for me right now is love my son."

"I can do that. I'll take Jack home now."

Diane returned to the waiting room and sat next to Jack. "Jack your mother wants me to take you home and so you can get some rest and I agree."

"But."

"You being here or at home won't change how long the operation will take. You need rest and the hospital only allows for one family member to stay over. Let's go home and I'll make you some dinner and we'll come back out here first thing in the morning."

He liked that she said home and not "the farm" like usual. "When you say cook do you really mean warm Momma's food up?"

She smiled, "Let's not split hairs funny man. There will be warm food in your belly that is all that matters."

He kissed her hand and stood. "Okay. But I'll drive myself. You have a test tomorrow."

"I'll drive, it's been a long day for you. Don't worry about me and my exams."

Jack went to the room to tell his mother goodbye, "Ma, Di and I are about to go home. Do you need anything before we go?"

"I'm fine. I'll call you with updates. Can we pray before you go?"

"Of course we can Momma."

They all held hands and bowed their heads, "Dear Lord, I know we've prayed so many times today, but I come to you once again. I know you're a powerful healer. I pray that you continue to guide the hands of the doctors as they remove that mass from my father. Please let the tumor be benign. Bless us all with the miracle of dad home and healthy soon. It is in the precious name of our Lord and Savior Jesus that we pray. Amen." They both kiss Rose on the forehead before leaving.

The drive home was quiet. Diane did not know what to say. Nothing she could say could soothe him. Once they were home, he went to finish up some of the minimum chores that needed to be done on the farm. When he came in he sat in the den and mindlessly flipped through channels while she finished cooking.

"Did you cook this?"

"Yes, and it's a first attempt so be nice. It won't taste like your mother's and I'm almost certain that it's edible."

He took her by the waist and kissed her. She felt so right. "Why didn't you just warm the leftovers up, darling?"

"I thought I'd use you as a guinea pig. If this is good I can be more of a help in the kitchen when your dad comes home. It'll give momma one less thing to worry about."

"Diane, just when I think I couldn't love you more you surprise me." He kissed her again. A sweet and loving kiss with just a hint of passion.

"Dinner will be cold if you keep kissing me like that."

Jack hesitantly took a bite of the food. "This is good Diane."

"Really? I've been taking mental notes but I wasn't certain how good it would be."

"It's really good, just like you."

They sat relatively quiet as they ate. He finished all the food on his plate and got seconds. Either he liked it, or he did not want to discourage her. Either way, she was greatly appreciative. Diane stood to do the dishes.

"Let me get those, you go study."

"You sure?"

"Positive. I'll clean this up and then I think I'm heading to bed."

Diane studied for a while then headed upstairs to call it a night. She was about to get in her bed, but left the room instead. Quietly she opened the door to Jack's room. He was sound asleep on his back. She tipped toed across the old squeaky floor and pulled the covers back. She was happy to see that he was sleeping in a t-shirt and boxers and not his birthday suit. She snuggled in close to his warmth and rested her head on his chest. He moved and wrapped his arm around her, pulling her closer.

"What are you doing in my bed Diane?" he asked without opening an eye.

"Shhh. Just sleep."

He tilted her chin up and kissed her. "If I weren't so tired, I'd take advantage of you."

"I'd let you." She lay her head on his chest and he pulled her in close until they drifted off to sleep.

THE NEXT MORNING JACK woke feeling more rested than the few hours of sleep he'd gotten. He knew that was because of the woman next to him. During the night they'd changed positions and her short- clad perfect, round butt was nestled snug against his intimate area which only enhanced his normal morning excitement. He wished New Year's Eve would get here soon. The sooner he got the ring on her finger, the sooner she'd walk down that aisle which meant the sooner he'd be able to give into his desire for her.

He tried to get up without disturbing her with no luck. She sat up and the covers fell down exposing her top half. Her nipples strained against the tank style pajama top she wore. She yawned with a big upper body stretch that made her shirt rise exposing her gently rounded stomach.

"Good morning."

Her voice made him realize he was staring. "Um, good morning."

"You want to head to the hospital?"

"After I feed the hogs, I'm going to come and get a quick shower and go."

"I'll help you."

"With the shower?" he asked with that dimple highlighting his grin.

"As if," she said much more lightly than she felt. "If I help you with the feeding you'll be done faster and we can get you to the hospital. Did Momma call?"

"Let me check." He looked at his phone and let out a little chuckle. "She sent a text, or probably had one of the nurses do it. She said the surgery went longer than expected, but they were able to remove the tumor successfully."

She wrapped her arms around him. "That's a blessing."

"It is. I'm so relieved." He returned the embrace and added a quick kiss to her lips. "Are you sure you want to help?"

"Of course I am. It's the least I can do."

Diane helped him feed the hogs. She wasn't certain she was of much help, but he was encouraging and appreciative for her novice attempt at hog farming. One tried to escape and she caught it, but Jack had to get it back in its pen between bursts of laughter. By the time they were done she was filthier than she'd ever seen Jack and possibly smelled worse than the animals. When they got back to the house he stopped her in the mud room.

"You better take that stuff off here. I don't want Momma to hurt you for getting her house dirty."

"Okay."

"Here, let me help."

He slowly removed every article of dirty clothing leaving her in just her bra and panties. His body responded immediately to the sight of her full breast barely contained by the bra. Her dark tips called to his mouth through the transparent lace. His hand could not resist and reached out to touch her hardened nipple.

"Why are you torturing me Jack?"

"Torture doesn't even begin to describe what seeing you like this does to me."

"You didn't need to see me like this. I am perfectly capable of undressing myself."

"Are you capable of showering by yourself as well?"

She was tempted to say she needed his help, but the phone rang saving her. Instead she said, "You should get that."

"Hello."

"Hi, Jack. I thought I'd missed you. Can you bring me a change of clothes? They offered me scrubs, but I don't trust their washing enough to wear them."

"Yes Momma. Diane will be dropping me off as soon as we shower?"

"Excuse me?"

"She helped me feed this morning since--" he was going to say since dad wasn't here but changed it to "so I could get there sooner."

"How'd she do?" The humorous smile could be heard in her voice.

Jack smiled at her, "Pretty good for a newbie."

"Diane's really special. Give her a kiss for me."

His body responded to the thought of kissing Diane, but he was certain that the kiss he had in mind wasn't the kind his mother meant. "I will Momma. See you in a bit." He hung up the phone.

He watched Diane head up the stairs. Her underwear barely covering her bottom giving him a beautiful view of smooth dark brown flesh as her rounded bottom swayed from side to side up the steps. He knew his shower would be colder and longer than normal.

AFTER HER LAST EXAM she rushed over to the hospital. Jack and Rose were both in Pete's room. Diane started to enter, but was stopped by one of the nurses.

"Only family is allowed to visit."

"I am family."

The nurse looked Diane up and down. "Really? You're his family?"

"Yes, I am his family."

"I don't see the resemblance."

"He's not my father. I am his son's girlfriend."

"Well there you have it. Son's girlfriend does not qualify you as a relative of the patient."

Diane was trying to hold tight to Jesus and not let some very choice words fly when Rose walked out.

"Diane you're here! What are you doing out here? Why didn't you come in? Jack's been waiting on you."

"I'm not a relative."

"According to who? You're family."

"Can you tell Nurse Ratchet that?"

"Mrs. Sloan. ICU rules are family only. She's only your son's girlfriend."

"If my son's best friend could come in earlier, she can come in now."

"Mrs. Sloan, I'm not sure which nurse let his friend in, but I'm sorry, I can't let her in."

"You were the nurse on duty when he came here a half hour ago. You didn't even question him. Did you assume that because he was white he was a relative?"

"I didn't see him go in or I would have stopped him."

"You were sitting right there behind the desk. So why don't you resume your seat and continue adding cellulite to your thighs with Twizzlers while you don't see her walk through that door."

"Mrs. Sloan! Insults aren't necessary."

"I agree, so stop insulting my intelligence by acting like you're enforcing a hospital rule and not being bigot," Rose said.

"I'm simply following the rules. You and this girl aren't worth getting written up for," the nurse said, speaking only to Rose.

"You should avoid ending sentences with prepositions, it makes you seem uneducated. This educated woman," Diane said pointing to herself, "would like you to get your supervisor before this situation gets any uglier."

"Is that a threat?"

"She was likely talkin' about your face." Rose's southern accent was getting stronger as she became more angry.

Diane held back her laugh and continued in her most poised tone. "Not at all. The ugliness was in reference to your treatment of me. At this time it can be settled with an apology and my entrance into the room. If it continues, the settlement will be for my pain and suffering and likely result in your termination. If you would please, get your supervisor."

"I am the head nurse."

Jack walked out of the room looking tired. He hadn't shaved and Diane felt bad for thinking the inappropriate thought of how sexy he was. He smiled when he saw her.

"What's going on out here? I heard raised voices."

"This hag isn't letting Diane in."

"Jack, Momma, you can go back in, I'll be in as soon as this is resolved with her supervisor."

Jack took Diane's hand and walked through the door into his father's room, "Whatever the problem is, it is now resolved."

Rose followed them into the room, but the nurse did not.

Pete was in the bed with many tubes and wires coming from him. She had only seen this stuff in movies. He was pale. So much different from the vibrant, joking man she'd come to know.

"Has he been awake since surgery?"

"No, but the doctors say his vitals are good."

"How are you doing?" she asked Jack.

He sat and pulled her down onto his lap. "Much better now that you're here. How was your exam?"

"I'm sure I passed."

"I'm sorry to distract you with this."

She took his face into her hands, "Jack, this isn't a distraction. The test was a distraction. I wanted to be here with you and your mom. I love you." She brushed her lips against his.

She was beyond amazing. He almost asked her to marry him right then and there. The only thing that stopped him was that they were in a hospital.

"MERRY EARLY CHRISTMAS DI. This is just a little something. It's not your real gift, just something you need." She unwrapped the small box and found a car charger for her cell phone. "I don't want you being stranded and falling for some sexy guy that stops to help you."

"Like that would ever happen. There was this one guy, but I don't know if I'd call him sexy."

"Oh really now?" He pulled her on his lap and kissed her until she sighed.

"So he wasn't sexy?"

"Well I guess there was something kind of attractive about him if you could see past the mullet." She slid off his lap and picked up a gift wrapped in elegant blue foil paper with a silver bow. "This is for you."

He unwrapped the box revealing a vanity plate that read "Hoosier" over an American flag. He smiled.

"Your real gift is underneath," she said with a look of anticipation in her eye.

He unwrapped the box but had no clue what he was looking at. "Um, thanks," he said trying to figure out what it was.

"It's a laptop recording studio," she reached for it, "you don't like it?"

He pulled it back from her. "I love it and I love you." He pulled her close for another kiss. "It's perfect because ever since I met you I've had a thousand songs in my head, and now I'll be able to share them with you."

"This is your real gift," he said handing her a box wrapped in snowman paper. Inside was a small wooden box with two hearts intertwined on it.

"It's beautiful."

"Open it."

She followed his instructions and opened the box. Inside was a silver bracelet with the words "follow your heart" engraved on the inside. Diane's eyes began to tear.

"Thank you. Having this on my wrist will make me miss you less over Christmas. Or I could just stay here."

"You missed Thanksgiving with your family. You should have Christmas with them."

"The food will be better here. For some reason my mother insisted on cooking this year."

"You're going home. I don't want your mother to hate me anymore than she already does."

"She doesn't hate you, she just doesn't like you. Welcome to the club, we have meetings monthly."

"Just promise you'll be back for New Year's Eve with me."

"Broke down cars and dead cell phones couldn't keep me away."

CHRISTMAS AFTERNOON DIANE WAS in the kitchen at her parent's house cooking when Amara came through the back door.

"Look at you. Is that an apron? You're so domesticated."Diane ran over and hugged her. "I missed seeing you in November.""You wouldn't give up meeting Jack to see me.""You're right, I wouldn't.""What has this man done to you? You're cooking and smiling at the mere mention of his name. Did you and him, you know?" She leaned closer to her friend to ask the question in confidence.Diane frowned and shook her head. "No, but it's not because I haven't wanted to. Every time he touches me I just want to-"Amara threw both hands up. "Stop! No is good enough for me. Spare me the details."Diane's phone rang. She wiped her hands on her apron and picked up the phone. Every tooth in her mouth seemed to show when she saw the name on the caller ID.

"That must be Jack."

"It is. Let me talk to him and I'll be right back." Diane passed Ryan as she exited the kitchen.

"Merry Christmas! I miss you so much Jack."

"Merry Christmas. I miss you more. I love you."

The sound of his deep voice made her heart flutter. Being away from him made her more certain of her feelings and easier to say the words. "I love you. How's your dad?"

"He's home. He was released this morning. The tumor was benign. Dad being home and healthy was the best gift."

"It was a Christmas blessing. I wish I were home too."

"You are home."

"You know what I mean."

"I don't. I'd like you to explain."

"I miss you."

Jack smiled. "You already said that."

"I know, but I haven't stopped missing you since the last time I said it."

"How are your folks?"

"Dad says mom's been cooking ever since their visit. She cooked breakfast, it was mostly edible."

"I love you Diane."

"You already said that."

"Well I still love you."

"I love you too."

"You'll still be back for New Year's Eve like we planned?"

"For the thousandth time yes."

There was a pause in the line indicating he had another call coming in. "Diane, I have to take this other call." "Do you have to?" She wondered who was so important he was rushing off the phone. "I do. I'll call you later. I love you." "I miss you."

Diane returned to the kitchen. Amara was leaning against the counter drinking bottled water.

"Where's Ryan?"

"He had to go. Was that Jack?"

"It was," Diane said, unable to keep the smile from breaking out across her face.

"Did I hear you say you love him?"

"You did." Diane waited for her friend to give her the same lecture that they hadn't known each other long enough like her mother had.

Amara studied her friend for a moment. "You really do love him."

"I do. I know it's irrational. I can't explain it with any logical explanation why I love him. It's just something I know."

"You must be going crazy. You're trying to do the impossible. You're trying to rationalize love."

"I just want to know that it's real."

"If you're happy, just be happy and don't try to figure out why."

Lena Hampton

Social Network

Diane Clark's status: Merry Christmas everyone.
There's nothing like being home for the holidays.
Jack Sloan, Magnolia Freeman, and 13 others like this.

Jack Sloan's status: It was a Merry Christmas and
it's going to be a great New Year.
Diane Clark, Cooper Smith and 21 others like this.

chapter 11

SHORTLY AFTER MIDNIGHT JACK SUGGESTED they leave the New Year's Eve party. He was really quiet during the ride back to the farm. Diane chalked it up to him being tired. He'd had a long week. She sat quietly next to him holding his hand. A couple of times he had to let her hand go to check incoming text messages. It was uncharacteristic for him to look at his phone while driving, let alone respond as he was doing tonight.

"You know that's illegal."

"What?" was his distracted answer.

"You aren't supposed to text and drive. Is everything okay?"

He smiled at her and took her hand back into his. "We'll see."

"I know the tumor was benign, but is something wrong with your dad?"

"He's good."

"Are we going to our spot?"

"Yep."

"Are you sure everything is fine?"

"I'm with you right?"

"Right."

"So everything is fine."

When they arrived at their spot in the field he helped her out of the truck in his usual fashion. Her body came alive as it slid against his. Maybe he was acting strangely because he wouldn't stop tonight when their bodies took control of their minds. Most people wouldn't think it was romantic to have their first time be in the back of a truck. But the back of this truck, with him, in this spot, where they fell in love, was possibly the most romantic setting.

Diane was in his arms with her head resting on his chest. He was far too quiet and it was making her heart race. Something was wrong and he wasn't telling her. She looked up at him and he looked normal. She laid her head back on his chest and placed her hand next to it. His somewhat abnormal behavior this evening combined with his elevated heart rate had her concerned about what was going on. Maybe their time apart had him realize his feelings were nothing more than infatuation.

"Di?"

"Yes?" she said nervously.

"I want to talk to you about something."

"Ok." Her voice was so soft it was almost inaudible. Her heart was now racing in anticipation of what he was about to say.

"Di, look at me."

Though she did not want to, she looked up at him. His eyes locked with hers. In the low light from the truck's cab his eyes still appeared to sparkle like a man in love.

"Di, do you love me?"

"Yes." She couldn't manage out more than one syllable,

He placed a sweet loving kiss on her lips. More gentle than the passion filled kisses they normally shared. His arms stayed around her locking her tightly against him.

"Do you know that I love you?"

"Jack, you're starting to scare me."

"How am I scaring you?"

"You've not been yourself all day."

"I've been myself all day." He was concerned that his nervousness had blown the surprise.

"No you haven't. You were unreachable for a couple of hours this afternoon and you were vague when I asked you where you were. Then you were antsy at the party, which you had us leave early. Then you bring me out here but don't say anything to me. I'm sitting here wondering if I'll have to perform CPR because your heart is beating out of your chest." She wiped the beginning of a tear from her eye. "Did you bring me out here to dump me?"

He laughed. Not a chuckle but a full robust laugh. A rush of emotions rushed through her at the sound. Anger was the one that came out first. She stood, needing to distance herself from him.

"Why are you laughing?" she yelled, standing over him with her hands on her hips.

His smile widened. "You'll understand shortly. Just give me one minute. Close your eyes and don't move."

"No, I want to see whatever it is coming."

"You're pretty cute when you're angry." He smiled at her. His smile was contagious, but she forced her face muscles to keep her mouth from curling up too. "Please, close your eyes Di."

"Fine." Diane stood in the back of the truck bed racking her mind as to what was going on. Music started playing. Through the haze of her emotions she realized the song was God Gave Me You, but it was Jack's voice. She felt the truck lower with the weight of Jack's return. Then his hands turned her around.

"Open your eyes." He was standing in front of her. She sensed there was something behind her and she began to turn around. "No, don't turn around."

"Jack, what's going on? I don't like this."

"Patience isn't your strongest virtue is it?"

She closed her eyes and took a deep breath. "No, it's not. Is anxiety a virtue because I have that in aces right now?"

"You know that I think it was more than just a coincidence that you and I met. I believe God had your car break down and put me on the road to help you because He intended us to be together. From the moment I saw you bundled up in your car I was drawn to you. By the end of that evening I knew you were for me. You're the most beautiful woman I've ever known, both inside and out. You're funny, and smart, and kind, and I could go on all night with your many virtues- patience not included. They say whoever you ring in the New Year with is the person you'll spend the year with. Di, I don't want to spend just the next year with you. I want to spend every year for the rest of my life with you."

He turned both of them around so that they switched places. He fell to one knee and that's when she saw Christmas tree lights in the field spelling out four words. "Will you marry me?" he said as if he were reading the words in the field.

Diane looked from him to the words in the field in shock. Jack was saying the words but what they were she wasn't sure because she was reminding herself to breathe. All she heard was mumble, mumble, short time since we met, blah, blah, long engagement, yadda, yadda, yadda. For the first time in a month, her heart and mind were in agreement. Moments ago when she thought he was ending things, she felt like her life was ending because she could not imagine life without him.

"Diane? Please say something to me."

She could not speak so she gave an imperceptible nod.

"Is that a yes?"

She just nodded again, a little more.

Jack stood in front of her. "If that's a yes can you please say the word so I can hear it?"

"Yes," she said softly "It's definitely yes." He slipped the ring on the ring finger of her shaking left hand. Unexpectedly she jumps up into his arms and wrapped her legs around his waist. He grabbed her bottom to hold her up as he stumbled back a couple of steps. She kissed him with every emotion in her body and he kissed back with equal passion.

"Thank you Diane."

"For what?"

"For saying yes." He kissed her again then placed her back on her feet.

"Is that you singing or am I going crazy?"

"That's me. I recorded it with my Christmas gift." He pulled out his phone to send a brief text message. Moments later there was an explosion in the sky and an eruption of color. He was happy she said yes because he didn't know if he had any more creative proposals in him and he knew he wouldn't stop asking until she said yes.

DIANE WAS SO EXCITED about being engaged that she dialed her mother's cell number on the brief ride from their spot to the house. Her mother didn't answer so she dialed her father. When her father didn't answer either, she remembered the time difference and figured they were probably still at church for watch night with their ringers off. She had to tell someone so she called her brother.

"Happy New Year sis!"

"Ryan, I'm going to get married!" she said not able to hold it in for another moment.

There was a long pause. "You and Alan worked things out?" he sounded confused.

"No. Jack proposed tonight."

"You said yes? You said yes to a man you've known a month? Are you crazy?"

"I'm related to you, so yes."

"Seriously Diane, do you know him well enough to marry him?"

"I expected this from mother, but not you." Diane let out a long sigh. She wanted him to be as excited as she was.

"It's just that I never said anything about Alan, even though I knew he was no good for you."

Her brother's words took her aback. He never said anything derogatory about her ex. "Just say congratulations and reserve judgment for when you meet him."

"Congratulations. I hope you know what you're doing. Does mom know?"

"I think she's still at watch-night service. Where are you? It's pretty quiet."

"Quiet celebration with a friend."

"A female friend?"

"Congrats Diane. I have to go, but call me if you need to after you talk to mom," her brother said ignoring her question.

"It sounded like he was super excited for you." Jack was concerned that without family support, Diane would cut her losses and call off the engagement. He was still kind of shocked she said yes.

Before Jack could put his truck in park, his mother was out the front door. The porch light made tears running down her face visible. The newly engaged couple rushed to her. Jack spoke first.

"Is something wrong with dad? Is something wrong?" He was not accustomed to seeing his mother cry.

"I'm just so happy. I heard fireworks! That means she said yes!" She hugged both of them, kissing their cheeks repeatedly. This was the joyous response they wanted.

"Congratulations. After the past couple of weeks we needed something like this to start the New Year off on a happy note."

Diane's phone rang. The joy went out of her like the air out of a balloon when she saw it was her mother's number. She walked into the welcoming heat of the house. "Happy New Year Mother."

"Happy New Year Diane. I wish I could have brought it in with my family, but both you and your brother had other plans."

"Yes Mother, I missed being with you too, but if I were there with you, I would have had to wait for Jack to propose."

"Are you telling me that boy proposed?"

"Yes."

"How did he take it when you said no?"

"I said yes."

"Are you pregnant?"

"No, Mother."

"Diane, why are you determined to throw your life away? Are you going to go live on a farm in the middle of nowhere and waste your law degree?"

"I'm not exactly in the middle of nowhere. I'm less than an hour from Indianapolis and even closer to Bloomington, but that's beside the point. I'm happy Mother and I want you to be happy for me too."

"I cannot be happy when you are making illogical choices that will negatively affect the rest of your life."

Diane walked into the dark den so that Jack and Rose wouldn't have to hear this conversation. She didn't want to bring down their moods on an occasion that should be joyous.

"Mother, this is not an illogical decision. I, in no way see how this will negatively affect my life."

"Diane, do not do this. Do not marry some white farmer on the rebound. If you do not want Alan, fine, you will find someone suitable. I cannot let you do this."

She couldn't stop the tears. She knew it was a long shot, but she'd hoped her mother would be happier. Even if she had to fake it. Jack came up behind her and put a supportive hand on her back. Even through the stress of this conversation his touch excited her.

"Mother, you didn't raise me to think race was an issue, but now that I'm engaged to someone not black and it's a huge issue."

"The fact that he is white is not ideal, but I have no issue with that. The issue is that he is just a farmer."

"I know you have your heart set on a doctor, but that's not going to happen. You act as if farming is drug dealing."

"No, farming is not drug dealing but he is likely growing marijuana in between rows of corn. He will get to continue being a farmer and you will be barefoot and pregnant and too busy cooking with lard to make use of the degrees your father and I have paid for."

"Mother, I know you don't support my decision, but it would mean a great deal to me if you would help me plan my wedding."

"I am not going to help you plan your demise."

"Hopefully by the time of the wedding you'll see that I'm happy and be there."

"I will only be there to object."

Diane had nothing more to say so she hung up. The possibility that that was the last conversation she'd have with her mother made her begin to cry without restraint. Jack wrapped his arms around her to absorb some of the pain she was feeling. When her cell phone rang, he took it out of her hand and answered it.

"Hello."

"Jack? It's Robert Clark. May I speak with Diane?"

"No disrespect sir, but she's still pretty upset from talking to your wife. I don't know if now is the best time to talk to her."

"Is that Daddy?" Diane said wiping tears from her face. "I want to talk to him." Jack handed her the phone.

"Hello, Daddy."

"I hear congratulations are in order." His voice was peppered with joy and concern.

"You don't feel the same as Mother?" Diane remained in Jack's arms with her head resting on his chest.

"I wouldn't have given him my approval when he asked for your hand if I felt the way your Mother did."

"He asked for my hand?" she said looking into Jack's blue eyes. He nodded and kissed her forehead. "Is there a dowry too?" she joked.

"There's no dowry, but you do have a small budget for your wedding. I'm pretty certain your cousin Magnolia will help make the budget seem ten times more."

"Thank you Daddy. I'll call Noli tomorrow. I love you."

"I love you too. So does your Mother. She'll come around. Hopefully not after it's too late to put her two cents in on the wedding."

"Happy New Year."

"You too sweetheart."

SOCIAL NETWORK

Diane Clark's relationship status changed to engaged to Jack Sloan.

Jack Sloan and 7 others like this.

Comments:

Amara Adams: Congrats. I'm not wearing an ugly bridesmaid's dress.

Noli Freeman: Congratulations. I'm happy for you cousin, but we obviously have some catching up to do.

18 More Comments

Jack Sloan's relationship status changed to engaged to Diane Clark.

Diane Clark and 13 others like this.

Comments:

Cooper Smith: I'll start planning the bachelor party. I'm happy for you man.

15 More Comments

chapter 12

THE NEXT DAY DIANE MADE all the phone calls she was too tired to make the night before. Her best friend Amara was excited, but didn't seem surprised. Her cousin Noli was confused that it wasn't Alan but happy and excited to come and help her plan. Jack took Diane out to eat to celebrate their engagement. She was nervous because she knew she would likely be the only black there. Despite Jack disproving many of her stereotypes she wasn't certain if he was the exception or the rule.

They sat at a bar height table near the bar. Shortly after ordering appetizers Jack excused himself to the restroom, kissing her cheek as he passed her. Diane looked around nervously and saw a stocky man with a bald head and a scraggly goatee wearing a hunting fatigue jacket and walking towards her. She grabbed her purse preparing to follow Jack if the situation was more than she could handle.

"I saw you here with Jack."

She nodded, not knowing how else to respond to his statement.

"Are you two a couple?"

She nodded again not certain her voice wouldn't betray her nervousness.

"Why?"

"Why not?" she said with more bravado in her voice than she felt. This conversation was going the same route as the one she had with Megan and she did not like it. With Megan she doubted that it would turn physical, but this man was unknown to her. This man was much larger than her so she needed an advantage. She grabbed Jack's beer bottle prepared to use it as a weapon against his head if needed.

"Well," he drawled taking the beer bottle out of her hand and drinking from it. Diane held her breath waiting for his next word. He smiled an easy smile and said, "Because you're too pretty for a schmuck like him. And probably smarter too, not that it takes much to be smarter than him. You could do much better."

Diane raised an eyebrow. "Can I?" she said relaxing just a tad.

"I know someone much better looking and a mile smarter."

She looked at his choice of grooming and wardrobe. "Really? Where?" she said pretending to look around for this potential new suitor.

"Oww, that hurts," he said putting his hand over his heart.

Before she could respond she heard Jack's deep baritone from behind her say, "We can arrange you hurtin'." He stood with his arms crossed looking quite intimidating and rather sexy.

"Do you really want me to embarrass you in front of your lady?" the hunter said with a smile.

"You ain't been able to whoop me since we were seven and you had help then," Jack said smiling. He grabbed the man's hand and pulled him in for one of those man hugs that kept their hands between them so their bodies wouldn't touch for fear they'd become instant homosexuals.

"Diane, this is Cooper. Cooper, this is my fiancée Diane."

Cooper hugged Diane without the benefit of the hand and forearm barrier. His embrace was warm but did not heat her like Jack's touch.

"I would say congratulations, but I think condolences would be more appropriate given who you're going to grow old with."

"Hey, where is my beer?" Jack said ignoring the slight. "Moving in on my lady is one thing, but taking my beer is unforgivable."

"Beer outranks me?"

"I know he doesn't have a chance with you. Beer doesn't have a choice."

"That's so sweet."

"Cooper is the mastermind behind the fireworks," Jack said.

This time Diane hugged Cooper. "You helped make the best night of my life memorable. Thank you Cooper."

"It was my pleasure. I just wish I had been the one to come along on the side of the road."

A walking stick with boobs and hair bleached to within an inch of its life came and stood between Jack and Diane. She stood with her back to Diane and placed a hand on Jack's bicep.

"Jacks, you forgot to come say hi." Her thumb began to rub back and forth across his arm. Diane could swear she saw his eye twitch.

"I didn't forget."

"That's so funny Jacks."

She faked hitting his chest then slowly let her hand run down his abs towards his waistband. Jack grabbed both of her hands and removed them from his body then moved to stand behind Diane.

"Misti, this is Diane. Diane, this is..."

"Misti, his wife." The word wife was emphasized to try and get a rise out of Diane, which it did, but that could not be discerned from looking at her face.

"Ex-wife. She's the reason I don't drink anymore. I don't always make the best decisions when alcohol is in my system. It makes me stupid. I lose bets and have to grow mullets or get married when the devil's poison is in my system."

"You remember that ex part when it's convenient for you," Misti said to Jack then looked Diane up and down. "So you must be Jack's flavor of the week."

"Jack, beer is alcohol," Diane said as she turned to Jack and ignored Misti as if the air hadn't just been knocked out of her. This was the first she'd heard of Jack being married. She'd learned from dealing with her mother to never show you're injured because that's when predators go in for the final kill.

"Beer is not alcohol." Jack says unsuccessfully trying to read Diane's tone and body language. "Beer is…" he trailed off.

"Beer is beer," Cooper inserted.

"Exactly, beer is not alcohol. Beer is beer"

Misti continued her train of thought disregarding the conversation over the classification of beer.

"I hope you know you're just a little experiment. He's just curious what chocolate tastes like but he has a thing for blonds. But I don't know if I'll take him back once he's diddled with something like you."

Misti referring to her as something instead of someone made her turn back to Misti. "Don't start none, won't be none Misti," Diane said imitating what she'd heard on the playground growing up.

"What does that even mean? I don't speak ghetto."

"It means I'm from the hood and your flat butt will have to be life lined out of here when I'm done with you. So it's best you leave while you're able to."

"I am so scared." Her tone held no fear, but her eyes did.

Diane threw back Cooper's shot and hopped off her bar stool, sending it loudly to the ground. She stepped toward Misti and looked down at her without saying anything for a few moments. Silence was intimidating because of the uncertainty of if it would be followed by more words or a fist to the face.

Misti took a step back and stumbled over the other bar stool.

"I don't need to fight you to get Jack back. I have other skills."

"With a name like Misti I'm sure you're quite talented on a pole." The other woman's name rolled off her tongue like something bitter. "You try to come between me and my man and I'll break your frail tail into so many pieces that they'll have to identify you by the serial number on your implants."

Diane heard Jack chuckle behind her. He put his hand on her waist and pulled her against him. He whispered in her ear loud enough for Misti to hear, "Darling, she's not worth it."

Misti had a look in her eyes like something from an episode of Criminal Minds. "I don't know what's gotten into you. That's it Jack, I'm done with you!"

"You promise?" Jack asked.

Misti stuck out her breasts and walked towards a table of guys that looked like they were allergic to soap and shampoo.

Diane turned around and took a step back away from Jack. "What on God's green earth was that? Motor oil?" Diane said pushing the shot glass away and gulping down her water to wash the taste out of her mouth.

"It was my whiskey," Cooper said. "I thought I was going to have to help Jack post bail for you."

"I'm glad she left. My mouth was writing checks my fist couldn't cash."

"You're quite the little actress, Di. I couldn't tell you didn't like that shot or that you weren't meaning what you were saying," Jack said as he took a step forward to close the distance Diane placed between them.

Diane took a step back again and glared at him as if he were a stranger. "Why didn't you tell me you were married Jack?"

"I'm going to go replace my shot," Cooper said knowing when to get out of dodge.

"It never came up."

"That's one of those things you should bring up. Sometime between hello and will you marry me you should have said 'I've been married before'."

"You're right. I didn't bring it up because that part of my life is something I wish to forget. You were already hesitant about me. I thought it would have been a deal breaker for you. I didn't want to give you any excuse to say no."

"Whether you being married before is a deal breaker or not should be up to me and not you." Diane kept her tone low and even so Misti couldn't revel in the damage the bomb she dropped caused.

"You're right."

"Jack, I'm starting to wonder if my mother was right. Maybe I'm crazy. I'm starting to wonder if I even know you."

"You're not crazy. You know me. Misti is part of who I was, not part of who I am."

"The truth is important to me."

"I didn't lie to you."

"Don't cross hairs," she cut off his defense. "I don't like being blindsided like that."

"You're right."

"You keep saying that. Do you really think I'm right or are you just patronizing me?"

"I mean it. You're right and I'm sorry." He pulled her in, hating the distance between them. It made him relax that she didn't resist. "Do you forgive me?" He smiled down at her.

"Stop smiling at me like that."

"Like what?" he said, smiling more.

"Like you're too sexy for me to be mad at you smile."

"Is it working?"

"Maybe a little."

"Do you forgive me?"

"I don't like secrets. We have to be honest with each other, even when we think it'll hurt. That's the only way we can make it as far as our parents have."

"So, you're still going to marry me?"

"It'll take more than bleach on top of silicone to run me off."

SOCIAL NETWORK

Diane Clark's Status: I'm not in the military, I don't believe in don't ask don't tell. Secrets always have a way to coming to light

Jack Sloan's Status: I hate when the past rears its over bleached head.

chapter 13

DIANE HAD TALKED TO HER father and brother several times over the next couple of weeks, but not her mother. It wasn't because she didn't want to talk to her but because her mother didn't want to talk to her. Diane was waiting at the Indianapolis Airport for her cousin's flight so they could start planning the wedding when her phone rang.

"Hello."

"Diane it is your Mother."

Diane didn't respond. She knew the only thing her mother wanted to come out of her mouth was that the engagement was off. Since that wasn't going to happen she waited for her mother to speak.

"Are you there Diane?"

"I am."

"Your father told me that his niece is coming to help you plan this...wedding."

Diane knew the hesitation before the word wedding didn't mean anything positive. "I'm at the airport now to get her."

"Why did you not ask me to help?"

"Because you don't want me to get married."

"Why would I want you to make a mistake?"

"You don't know Jack well enough to say marrying him is a mistake."

"I do not know Jack? You cannot know that boy. Right now I am not sure if I know you. Diane, if he is some itch you need to scratch, scratch it but use caution and do not commit the rest of your life to him."

"I can't believe you just said that. I love him. He loves me. We are getting married. If you're not on board, then why did you call? In fact, until you can respect my decision you don't need to call me."

Catherine paused before she spoke so she could control her voice and remove the quiver of hurt from it. "I will get 'on board' as you say, but I am your mother and love you far too much to watch you make a mistake without trying to steer you away from it."

"You didn't question my previous engagement. In fact you encouraged it even after he was unfaithful."

"If you are referring to Alan, you were with him for over three years before you got engaged. Have you thought about when you will have the wedding?"

"In about one month. It depends on how quickly Noli, Rose and I can get the arrangements together."

Again, Catherine was hurt that she was excluded from the planning while Jack's mother is a part of it.

"Are you pregnant?"

"No mother."

"Since there is no pregnancy, can you have a longer engagement?"

"We want a short engagement Mother."

Catherine hated the way Diane said the word Mother like it was an indictment for a war criminal. "In that case, what can I do to help with preparations? Perhaps I can find a reception hall."

"Won't that be difficult to do from up there?"

"What do you mean Diane?"

"We're getting married down here."

"Are you trying to kill me?" Catherine couldn't control her voice as it rose an octave.

"Of course not. When you said you weren't even going to attend, we decided to have it here."

"Between Magnolia and Rose, it sounds like you do not need me. If something comes up, and I can be of assistance, let me know."

"I will do that. Thank you."

"You are welcome." Catherine heard a touch of surprise in her daughter's voice. It was obvious to her that Diane didn't understand she only wanted her to be happy.

"I see Noli Mother. I have to go."

"Tell Magnolia I said hello."

DIANE PULLED UP TO where her cousin was standing with several bags. Her cousin appeared to have lost even more weight in the months since they'd last seen each other shortly after the funeral for Noli's parents. Her cousin was understandably having difficulty dealing with her parent's sudden death at the hands of a drunk driver a little over eight months ago.

"Princess Di," Noli exclaimed when Diane got out of the car. Her cousin had given Diane the nickname because she often referred to her uncle's wife as the Queen of Mean.

"Noli!" The two embraced for a long moment. No matter how much time passed between seeing each other it seemed like no time had passed. "How much did you pay in baggage fees?"

"Too much. These bags have been across the country and around the world with me." Noli had been quite a nomad since shortly after her parent's funeral, trying to outrun the pain of them being gone. "Each place I've visited has added another bag."

"Will you be going home after the wedding?"

Noli paused and her eyes watered for a moment. "I doubt it. Uncle Robert is taking good care of the house."

"Are you ready to plan a wedding?" Diane said changing the subject before they started crying at the airport pick-up lane.

"I'm ready to plan an urban-chic-country wedding for you and this random guy you met on the side of the road."

"He's not some random guy. Wait, did you say urban-chic-country?"

"Exactly. As soon as I get settled in the hotel, I'll come show you what I already have in mind."

"About the hotel, Jack's mom said no family of hers was staying in a hotel when there was an empty bed in her house. I love you, but I didn't want to fight that battle for you. Especially since I doubt I could win."

"Not staying in a hotel will be a good change. Plus I'll get a chance to catch up with my favorite cousin."

"I have a lot of ideas for the wedding."

"That's good, but I don't want this wedding to have you so preoccupied you won't have time to study for the bar exam."

"You and Momma are going to get along just fine. She said the same thing."

"When did you start calling Aunt Catherine, Momma?"

"I was talking about Rose, Jack's Mom."

"Wow you're moving fast. Calling his mother, Momma. Marrying him after just a month."

Diane sighed. "Please don't start Noli. I thought you'd be happy for me."

"I am very happy for you. I can't wait to meet Jack because he must be something special. I'm just amazed.

I'm confused too. This is just so, so, spontaneous. It sounds like something I would do, not you."

"You rubbed off on me. I guess I've changed. "

"I'm sure I wasn't the only one rubbing on you. I'm sure Jack's done plenty of..."

"Noli, that is so inappropriate!"

Noli laughed. "And Diane is back."

As they pulled up Rose was walking onto the porch. Noli got out of the car and reached her hand out to the women smiling before her.

"You must be Mrs. Sloan, it's so good to meet you. Thank you for letting me stay here."

"You're just like Diane, trying to shake hands and calling me Mrs. Sloan. Come here." She wrapped her up in a warm hug. "Oh Magnolia, did you catch a bug or something while you were traveling? You're so thin. Or did you get tired of hotel food? You've probably seen more hotels than a high class hooker."

"I, um, I have seen a lot of hotel rooms." Noli leaned into Rose's embrace. "Please call me Noli. Magnolia is my great grandmother."

"And you call me Rose. Are you hungry?"

"No, I ate on the plane."

"Diane, let that fiancée of yours get the bags. Magnolia, you come on in and eat. Peanuts and soda are not a meal."

A few minutes later Magnolia sat at the kitchen table eating the best biscuit she'd ever had when Jack walked in carrying a few of her bags followed by another guy carrying the rest up to her room. The two men returned down stairs and it was easy for Noli to tell which was Jack from the way he looked at Diane. Noli understood why her cousin was rushing to the altar. If a man looked that good and looked at her that way, she'd be saying 'I do' too.

"Noli, this is Jack."

"Nice to meet you Jack." Noli went to shake his hand but he pulled her into an embrace much like his mother did.

"Noli, thank you for coming to plan our wedding," Jack said then released her from the embrace.

"I'm happy to be here."

"Noli, this is my buddy Cooper."

"It's nice to meet you." Cooper's voice made Noli want to sigh. She attempted to just wave hello, but was once again pulled into an embrace. Jack's hug was warm, but Coop's was electrifying and lasted a little longer.

"Noli, Cooper has volunteered a space at his place for the wedding," Diane said. "Maybe after dinner we can go check it out."

"I was hoping to spend some time with you after dinner," Jack said smiling at Diane.

"You two spend some time together," Magnolia said. "If I can borrow your car I can go look on my own."

"It can be easy to get lost, I can take you over to look at it, if you want," Cooper said.

"Sure, that sounds good."

DIANE SAT QUIETLY NESTLED in Jack's arms in the back of the truck out at their spot. Noli was with Cooper looking at the structure on his property that might be used for the reception.

"Di, dad said he spoke with you about transferring the farm to me."

"He did. He told me he wants to travel with your mom."

"I've been pretty much running the farm for the last couple of years anyway," Jack said.

"I told him I'd draft the transfer documents if he agreed to stop talking about grandchildren," Diane said with a smile.

"Di, how many children do you want?"

"I don't know. I've never really thought about it."

"You were engaged, didn't you two talk about how many children you wanted?"

"We both agreed we'd get our careers underway before we started a family. I guess we thought we'd cross that bridge down the road."

"Do you even want children?"

"I do. The thought of being someone's Mother scares me though."

"You'll be a great Mother. You're kind and caring and there are so many things that will make you a wonderful Mother."

"Thank you. I do want to have a child or two." she said this time with a little more certainty. "I want to have your children. You'll be a great Dad. How many do you want?"

"As many as you'll give me. I was awfully lonely being an only child."

"That's obvious. If you had brother's maybe you would have chosen better friends," Diane said with a laugh.

"Hey give Cooper a break."

"We digress. Are you okay with waiting a year or two for babies?"

"I don't mind as long as I get to practice that entire time."

"You could practice now, but you're being so old fashioned."

"My mother has a name for girls like you," he went in for a kiss and she pulled back.

"Does your mother think I'm easy?"

"I'm fairly certain she thinks you've given up the cookies. I think she thinks you've given in to me. She has no clue that you're the one trying to get in my pants every chance you get."

She moved on top of him and straddled him. "Why won't you give in? We'll be married soon. Doesn't the engagement come with some benefits?"

"You've waited twenty-five years, what's a few more weeks?"

"A few more weeks of you walking around here looking like you do and talking with that deep voice will be torture." She let her finger trace the skin above his t-shirt's collar.

He took her hands into his to halt the assault to his senses.

"In a couple of years, will you be beautiful with a round belly regardless of if your career is exactly where you expect it to be?" His voice took a serious tone.

"I can't promise that Jack. Two years is both a lot of time and not much time. Anything can happen or I could still be shuffling papers."

"I know, but having children isn't the end of your career."

"Jack, I've already had to rethink my entire career path by marrying you. I don't know how much that will hinder me being partner someday?"

His face became hard and his eyes cold as he stared into her brown eyes. "Do you think marrying me is a hindrance? It's not too late to back out."

"I didn't mean it like that at all. Jack, being your wife is more important than a partnership. I was just saying that being so rural limits my options. I won't have as many opportunities."

"Would just being my wife be enough for you?"

Her heartbeat accelerated as anger erupted in her. "You want me to give up being a lawyer to be a barefoot and pregnant farmer's wife?" she grunted out. He held her on his lap when she tried to move.

"I didn't say that. I was asking if it came down to you just being my wife, would that be enough. Would I be enough for you or would you resent me? I know I'm asking you to give up a lot, but I can't leave here. I can't ask my father to not retire and I can't let a farm that's been in the family for generations be sold to some big farming conglomerate."

"I'm not asking you to give up the farm. I love you for being so dedicated to your family but you don't understand the sacrifices I'm making to be with you."

"You're right. I don't know anything about sacrificing dreams for this farm." He gently pulled her up from his lap. "We need to get back to the house." They had no schedule, but the conversation was heading in a direction neither of them wanted it to go.

"I'm sorry Jack that was a stupid thing to say." She realized that he'd given up dreams that would never be achieved. She was just giving up the way her dreams would be achieved.

He did not respond. Instead he got up and got into the truck without helping her in. He had always helped her in. This was the first time he did not. The drive back to the house started off quiet. He'd turned up the radio to discourage her from talking. She had never seen Jack upset with her. She did not like the way he shut down and shut her out. She looked out the window so he could not see her tears fall.

"I'm really sorry Jack. I love you," her voice was soft and shaky.

He looked at her. She looked scared and sad. Her smile was a futile attempt. Even in the darkness her eyes were wet and her cheek looked moist.

He stopped the truck and gave her a full smile. "I love you too Diane. I'm so sorry I snapped like that. It wasn't about you. Misti and I got a divorce after she aborted our child without my knowledge."

Diane's large brown eyes stared at him for a moment. "Oh Jack. I don't know what to say. I…" she trailed off truly at a loss for words.

"When I first moved to Nashville she followed me and was itching for a ring with the promises of love and family. Instead I got infidelity and lies. I guess she just wanted her hands on my money."

"What money?"

"I got a little over a hundred grand from my parents. It was supposed to be for college, but they gave it to me when I decided to pursue a music career."

"That is a whole lot of money for an eighteen year old."

"Especially one blinded by the prom queen's confessions of love. I married her and she ran through the money as fast as she could. Well, when I got the record deal, she was in hog heaven. She had started house and car shopping. Then Dad got sick. I came home but she stayed in Nashville and refused to come home. She thought if she stayed there I'd miss her enough to return and sign the contract. When I told her that I was not coming back but planned on moving home, she was enraged."

Diane placed her hand on top of Jack's.

"About a month after that, she sent me an ultrasound and a note that said I would have kept your baby if you came back. When I called she said she was not going to let a baby of a nobody farmer ruin her body or her life. She was going to use her assets to get somebody that had goals and a future. I filed for divorce that day."

"What brought her back here?"

"She tacked on to this up and coming singer that spent more money on coke than he did her. Eventually she came home but she wasn't the big fish in this small pond anymore. She started coming back around me when she figured out me and this farm was better than a dead end job in a small town." He let out a halfhearted chuckle. "One time, Momma shot at her."

"She did?" Diane said surprised that the loving woman would wield a gun at another person.

"Yea she did. She was willing to do jail time if it meant Misti was six feet under. Momma wanted a house full of children but only had me. She was looking forward to a house full of grandchildren."

"Jack I'll have as many of your babies as I can whenever you want. I love you."

"I love you too. We can wait on the children, but please never cry again."

"I know, Mother says I'm not a pretty crier." Diane wiped at her eyes again.

"You're always beautiful. Even when you cry. I don't want you to cry because it hurts too much to know I'd caused you to hurt and made you cry."

"I wasn't crying because you hurt me, I was crying because I thought I hurt you. What I said was thoughtless."

"We did it," Jack said smiling.

Diane looked confused. "What did we do?"

"Survived our first fight." He leaned towards her. He cupped her face in his hands and kissed her. "I love you Diane."

"I love you Jack."

SOCIAL NETWORK

Message from Cooper Smith to Jack Sloan: What's the 411 on Noli? Is she single?

Message from Jack Sloan to Cooper Smith: I believe she is. Why? Keep in mind Diane is very protective of her cousin.

Diane Clark's status: I didn't realize how much I missed my cousin until I saw her.

Noli Freeman likes this.

chapter 14

DIANE TURNED THE CORNER INTO the living room and stopped in her tracks. Jack stood before her in a suit, but his shirt was still undone and the tie was on the back of a chair. This was her first time seeing him in something other than jeans. He wore jeans well, but the way the suit draped over his muscles was devastatingly sexy.

"If you don't put your coat on we'll be late."

"We have time."

"Not if you keep looking at me like that, while you're standing there in that dress looking like that."

She twirled. "So you like."

"Oh darling, I love." He said picking up his tie.

"No tie." She traced her finger along his chest exposed by the open collar of his shirt. His skin was smooth, warm and hard. Her mouth watered and her lips tingled as she thought of kissing him there. "I like the way you look without it."

"Your mother won't go for no tie look."

"Is it my mother..." She planted a kiss on his neck giving into temptation. "...or me..." She kissed a little lower as her hand ran up his chest. His breath caught. "...that you want..." She opened her mouth and lightly sucked on his neck. "...to be happy?" She bit him gently by his collarbone.

"You," he said, throwing the tie. He grabbed her by the waist and pulled her close to him. He kissed her gently on her lips. He returned the kiss to her neck, then moved up and sucked on her ear. Then he whispered, "You look beautiful tonight."

"You look so sexy in that suit. I can't wait until tomorrow night."

"Me either darlin', but if we don't get out of here your mother will kill us and there won't be a tomorrow for us."

Catherine got her way about two things, the rehearsal dinner was at an overpriced restaurant in Indianapolis and Diane was to spend the night in an equally overpriced hotel in the city. Jack stood with his arm around Diane's waist as they enjoyed cocktails with their close friends and family. Diane suddenly went rigid in his arms. He followed her glare and noticed a tall, well dressed black man.

"She did not!" Diane growled out.

Jack had never heard Diane sound so angry. He followed where her eyes were looking.

"Who is that?" Jack asked, but Diane had already broken their embrace and started across the room.

As Diane went off looking for her mother, Jack reasoned that the man must be Alan. He strolled calmly in his direction.

"You must be Alan." Jack didn't bother to reach his hand out.

"You must be Jake."

Jack ignored the fact that Alan had called him by another name because he knew it was done to get a reaction out of him. "I hope you're here to wish Diane and me luck."

Alan smirked. "It's Diane and I."

"It's Diane and me. What it's not is Diane and you. What are you doing here?"

"I was invited."

"You weren't invited by anyone that could invite you, but I'm glad you're here. I wanted to thank you for being foolish enough to cheat on Diane. If you hadn't, I wouldn't be escorting you out of my rehearsal dinner tonight."

"Are you afraid you'll be left at the altar once she talks to me? Because I'm not leaving. "

"You're leaving. The only thing I'm afraid of is not having bail in time for the wedding."

"Is that a threat?"

"He's not threatening you, he's warning you." Cooper said standing behind Alan with his arms folded across his broad chest. "I mean it's pretty brave for you to come here."

"I wouldn't expect any less than this kind of greeting from a couple of good ol' boys."

"This ain't a good ol' boy greeting. Good ol' boys greet pretentious metro-sexuals from the city with their fists." Cooper said taking a step closer to Alan.

"I think we'll let Diane decide if I stay or leave." Alan said.

"I can speak for my fiancée. She doesn't want you here."

"Listen, you were just the first thing to come along to help her get over me. I care about Diane and I don't want her to turn the rebound guy into her husband."

"You may care about Diane, but I love her. She hasn't thought about you since she met me."

"That's not exactly true," Diane said joining the three men. She took Jack's hand for comfort and to inhibit it from punching anyone. The testosterone level was at a critical point. "I stopped thinking about him before I met you. Meeting you made him not even a memory."

"Diane, can we talk alone?" Alan asked, emphasizing the last word.

"No."

"Fine, if you want to talk in front of these yahoos, we can. Don't do this, don't throw your life away. You could be so much more with me in Chicago than you could even dream about with him. You don't even know him."

"I've achieved love and happiness with him. That's something I never had and could never see with you. I know him better than I ever knew you. I know he'd never have some other woman bent over the kitchen counter. I know that my happiness is important to him. I know that when he says he loves me it means he loves all of me, just as I am."

"There does seem to be more of you to love. Did you turn to food to deal with losing me?" Sadly the genuine concern in his voice was for her dress size and not for her.

Diane stepped in front of Jack to prevent him from defending her. "I turned to food to deal with my barely controllable sexual desires."

Words of love and faithfulness hadn't gotten to him as much as reminding him how sexually inadequate she found him. "I doubt an ice princess like you would melt for some backwoods hick farm boy."

"I think it's best that you leave before I go full hick farm boy on you," Cooper said. If there was going to be a fight it would be him doing the fighting. As best man it was his obligation to not only take a black eye in the groom's place but also go to jail so that the groom made it down the aisle the next day.

Perhaps it was too much confidence in his workouts, but Alan didn't move.

"Diane, do you really think you'll be happy living in the middle of nowhere? Why did you even bother with law school? If you were going to just throw away your degree you should have just come with me to Chicago and it would have been you bent over the counter."

The thought of Alan touching her made her want to gag. It made Jack and Cooper both take a step towards Alan. Noli had joined them and placed her hands on Cooper's chest to stop him.

"He's not worth it."

"She's right. He's not worth it," Diane said pulling Jack back by the arm. "He's leaving any way."

"Don't come crying to me when you've realized the mistake you've made," Alan said gesturing towards Jack.

Cooper had had enough if no one else had and pushed Alan towards the door. "Let me show you out." He gave another push making Alan stumble.

"I'm so sorry Jack. I'm sorry mother invited him here to ruin tonight. I still need to find her." Diane's voice was part sadness, part anger.

"Don't be too hard on your mother. She loves you." Jack hugged her to reassure her that everything was okay.

Diane walked around for a few minutes but didn't find her mother. She saw her brother standing on the deck with a drink in his hand.

"Have you seen your mother?"

"I saw Dad and her talking out front. He seemed more upset with her than you."

"I can't believe she invited Dr. Insincere to my rehearsal dinner."

"I can. She thinks you're making a mistake and thought you needed to see Alan again to come to your senses and leave Jack."

"Well that backfired. Seeing him confirmed how wrong he was for me and how right Jack is for me."

"I don't think that you should be with Alan. Though I hate to agree with Mother, it does seem kind of fast."

Diane let out a long breath. "You too Ryan? Jack and I love each other. We're both certain that our future is together, and don't feel the need to wait." She turned to go.

Ryan touched her arm. "If you're sure, you shouldn't wait." Ryan took a sip of his drink and sat on the steps. "Trust me, you'd regret it if you let love slip through your fingers."

Diane sat next to him, studying his profile for a moment. "Did you let love slip away?"

"Something like that, but we're not talking about me right now."

"No, we're talking about mother. She would never interfere with her favorite like this."

His eyebrows raised. "You think I'm mom's favorite? You're crazy."

"Crazy? You can do no wrong in her eyes."

"She doesn't care enough to notice if I'm doing wrong. I could bring home a meth addict and she'd say it could be worse, she could be a crackhead."

"Well if I came home on meth she'd tell me it was bad for my teeth and I should use crack to lose some weight." They both laughed.

"I would argue, but you might be right." He chuckled as he imagined his mother saying that. "Don't let mom talk about your weight. You look good. You look happy too."

"I wish I could say the same about you. You don't look too happy." She paused hoping he'd voluntarily tell her what was going on, "Amara doesn't seem too happy when she sees you. Is something going on with you two? "

He looked away from her, afraid she'd be able to read his eyes and know the truth. "What makes you say that?"

"I've seen you talk to her with less than amicable results and I've seen her avoid you like the plague."

For a moment it looked like he was going to open up, but instead he said, "You need to ask her not me."

"I did. I asked her why I had to dodge daggers every time she looked at you and she said it was my imagination."

"Then I guess it's just your imagination Sis."

"Imagination smagination. If you don't want me to know, I'll drop it, for now. But, I'll tell you what I told her, you two play nice and smile real pretty in my pictures then feel free to carry on with the imagined tension."

"How's this Sis?" he smiled an overly cheesy smile that made her laugh.

Ryan's goofy smile fell when he noticed Amara walk out with Noli and a couple of Diane's other friends. He quickly plastered on the fake, but believable smile that he'd perfected. Diane's smile fell when she saw a cheap veil and a hot pink banner in her friends' hands.

"Diane, we have to go celebrate your last night as a maiden," Noli said placing the veil on her head.

"You deserve a drink or two after that party crasher."

"If I tried to say no, you'd just force me to go?"

"Yes," the women said in unison.

Diane quickly found Jack. "They're making me go party."

"Cooper is making me do the same thing. Have fun. Don't drink too much."

"You don't make any bets with Cooper."

He bent down and placed a kiss on her neck until she sighed. "The next time I see you, you'll be walking down the aisle," he whispered in her ear.

Just as he began to kiss her again, Amara pulled her away.

"You two will have plenty of time for that tomorrow and for the rest of your lives, we only have a couple of hours to get drunk and make fools of ourselves."

JACK HAD JUST WAVED Cooper good-bye and had one foot on the step to his house when headlights turned on illuminating the front porch. The light blinded him so that it took a few moments for him to recognize who it was.

"Exes," he muttered under his breath.

"I need to talk to you Jack."

"Not tonight Misti." Jack inserted his key into the door and opened it.

"But Jack..."

Jack shut the door but could still hear what sounded like the words pregnant and father. He was sure this was a last ditch effort to ruin his relationship with Diane, but he thought it would be better to hear it now, then her try to show up during the ceremony. He stepped out and shut the door behind him before she could attempt to come in.

"You have three minutes Misti."

She smiled and cocked her head to the side. "We've never been able to finish anything in three minutes Jacks." She ran her hand along his chest. "You look quite handsome."

Jack snatched her hand off of him. "Misti, you now have less than two minutes so get to the point."

"Fine." She stepped into the light and stood sideways. For the first time Jack could see the roundness of her midsection. "I'm pregnant. You're the father. We're having a baby. Was that to the point enough for you?"

"You may be pregnant, but I'm not the father."

She placed her hand over her stomach. "This happened Halloween night."

"I don't remember parts of that night, but I doubt we did anything that resulted in that," he said pointing to her round belly.

"You doubt that it happened, but you ain't sure we didn't rekindle the flame. We were as hot as ever, I don't see how you could forget."

"I can't forget something that never happened."

"It happened. And this is our baby. I just wanted you to have all the facts so you can decide if walking down the aisle tomorrow is in the best interest of our child."

"I'm walking down the aisle tomorrow and marrying Diane. I don't believe that child is ours because I don't believe we even kissed, let alone made love that night."

"You may not believe it, but we made love that night."

"If anything happened that night, it was just sex, it had nothing to do with love. You killed any love I may have had for you a long time ago. You have to go. Your two minutes are up."

"Are you still going to marry her when I'm carrying your child?"

"We both know you're like Wal-Mart, open anytime to anyone with a couple of bucks. I doubt that you know who the father is. I need more proof than just your word that I'm the father."

There was a flash of hurt in her eyes, but her words were full of anger. "You may still want to marry her knowing I'm carrying your child, but I bet she won't want to say I do to you knowing your bastard child will be a frequent visitor to her happily ever after."

Jack stepped closer to her and stared down at her with menacing eyes. "You don't say anything about this to her or anyone else until you have proof that's my child. It wouldn't be good for you. I won't let you ruin Diane's day or screw with my life again."

Misti just stared up at him for a moment before looking away. "Fine, I won't say anything. It'll be our little secret, for now. But will your marriage survive the truth coming to light? Oh, and how will she react when she knows you knew but didn't tell her?"

"Misti. Go. Now." He stepped around her and went to the house without turning to see if she left. The house was quiet, accept the increasing sound of conflict in his head.

Before he could head upstairs there was a knock at the door. "Misti, go before Momma pulls out her gun again," he said flinging the door open to see Cooper and not Misti standing there.

"I thought that was her car I passed. That's why I came back. What did she want?"

Jack stepped back out and took a seat on the top step. "She's pregnant and she says the baby's mine."

Cooper joined Jack on the step. "When did this happen?"

"I don't think it did, but she says it happened Halloween. I just remember waking up with a massive hangover and not much memory of the night before."

"It's really convenient she tells you the night before your wedding."

"She thought it would make me call it off."

"Are you going to tell Diane?"

"When, tonight while she's drunk or tomorrow right before she vows to love me forever?"

"Neither of those are ideal. If I were you, I would wait until after the wedding, but don't keep it secret for too long."

His friend was right. Diane hated secrets. But he'd take his chances of her being mad later. Especially since he had major doubts about the paternity of Misti's child.

SOCIAL NETWORK

Diane Clark's status: I'm so excited. Tomorrow I will be Mrs. Diane Sloan.

Jack Sloan, Noli Freeman, and 28 others like this.

Comments:

Jack Sloan: I'm more excited.

Noli Freeman: It's going to be a beautiful wedding.

Ryan Clark: I'm happy for you both.

17 More Comments

Jack Sloan's status: Tomorrow I'll be the luckiest man on earth because Diane Clark will become Diane Sloan.

Diane Clark, Cooper Smith, and 36 others like this

Comments:
Diane Clark: I'm the lucky one
Jack Sloan: We're both lucky.

chapter 15

STANDING OUTSIDE THE DOORS TO the sanctuary with her arm looped through her father's, Diane took a deep steadying breath. She wasn't nervous about marrying Jack, but she was afraid she'd trip, or that her mother would stand up and object, or Misti would burst through the doors on Alan's arm.

She looked up at her father. He was smiling. "You look lovely Sweetie," he said to her.

"Thank you, Daddy. You look awfully handsome yourself. Why haven't you asked me if I'm moving too quickly like everyone else?"

"I knew I wanted to marry your mother before the first date. There was no logical explanation, I just knew. When Jack asked me for your hand, he said he knew he wanted to spend the rest of his life with you, and I believed him."

"I still can't believe he actually asked you for my hand."

"I like that he did. That's another reason I don't doubt your decision. I know you're marrying a good man."

When the doors opened the first thing Diane saw was Jack standing there in his tux with his hands at his side. The sun was streaming through the stained glass windows on him. All thoughts of possible calamities left her mind when she saw him. Diane could not tell what a single flower or ribbon looked like. She only saw Jack.

WHEN THE DOORS OPENED, Diane walked through dressed in a simple white satin sleeveless gown that hung to her every curve. The design accentuated all her features making her look beautiful and sweet and sexy all at once. Jack forgot to breathe until she reached him.

"You look so incredibly beautiful," Diane whispered.

"I think that's supposed to be my line," Jack smiled. "But beautiful doesn't begin to describe how wonderful you look."

"Ladies and Gentlemen, family and friends, we are gathered here together to celebrate the union of Jack and Diane before God," the pastor began. "I've only known this couple for a short while. As I've come to know them, I've seen love. Not just love for each other, but love for God as well. They would like to express their love for each other before the vows. Jack, you're first. Please turn to your bride."

"Diane, our meeting was not coincidental, but a destiny chosen by God. When I stopped to help you, I thought you had the most beautiful brown eyes I'd ever seen. Of course I could only see your eyes since you were so wrapped up in that scarf. I love you because your smile is my comfort and your eyes are the beacons to light my way. Diane, God answered my prayer for love with you. It may have taken you twenty minutes of stubbornly sitting in a freezing car to realize God had sent me to answer your prayer for help. I will thank Him in every prayer that you said yes to our first date and to spending the rest of your life with me. I will praise God every day by loving you with all that I am."

Diane wiped at the tears that his vows caused. Her hands were shaking in his. "We had a deal, you weren't supposed to make me cry again."

"Sorry." He wiped the tear that was falling down her cheek.

"I should have gone first because I don't know if I can follow that." Diane took a deep breath. "Jack, when you first pulled up behind my stranded car my heart began to race and it's never beat the same since. At first it beat with fear, but just one of your smiles turned my fears into comfort and made my heart skip a few beats. If I am sad, you make me happy, if I am happy, you make me ecstatic. Jack, with you, God answered a prayer I hadn't even thought to pray yet. You are everything I never knew I needed and everything I could ever possibly want. Saying I love you seems insufficient to express how I feel about you."

The pastor read a verse from the Bible and blessed the rings. Diane and Jack barely heard a word as they gazed into each other's eyes. "Jackson Sloan, do you take Diane Clark to be your wife?"

It took a moment for Jack to realize he'd been spoken to. "I do. I most certainly do. I take you Diane, to be my wife, loving you now and as you grow and develop into all that God intends. I will love you when we are together and when we are apart; when our lives are at peace and when they are in turmoil; when I am proud of you and when I am disappointed. I will honor your goals and dreams and help you to fulfill them. From the depth of my being, I will seek to be open and honest with you. I say these things believing that God is in the midst of them all. I give you this ring as I give myself to you, with love and affection."

Jack slipped the diamond band onto Diane's shaking finger. She repeated the vows, expressing the depth of her love and taking Jack as her husband. She slipped the simple white gold band onto his finger. Though the church was full, it seemed that they were the only two people there.

"Now that Jack and Diane have given themselves to each other, before God, by the promises they have exchanged, I pronounce them to be husband and wife, in the name of the Father, and of the Son, and of the Holy

Spirit. Amen. Jack," the pastor paused for a long moment before finishing, "you may kiss your bride."

Diane wrapped her arms around Jack's neck as he pulled her to him by her waist. He lowered his mouth to hers. The kiss lasted until they were out of breath. He rested his forehead on hers.

"You're my wife," he whispered.

"I know. And you're my husband." she whispered back. "You know what that means," she said with a wink.

"MOMMA THAT CAKE IS beautiful!" Diane said to Rose.

"I was hoping you liked it."

"I love it."

"It is a very lovely cake Mrs. Sloan." Catherine Clark said.

"Thank you," Diane said with a laugh knowing her mother was talking to Rose, but unable to suppress her champagne induced giddiness at being Mrs. Sloan.

Catherine smiled at her daughter's joke. "Listen, Diane." Her mother's tone took some of the giddiness away. "You seem happier than I have ever seen you before. It is obvious how much Jack loves you."

That was the closest thing to an apology that Diane had ever received from her mother but their conversation was cut short by the DJ announcing their first dance and Jack was by her side to take her into his arms. They had agreed on Endless Love. The song began to play but instead of the usual musical arrangement, it was just a guitar. Diane lost her step when she heard Jack's voice come over the speakers. She looked at him in shock and her eyes began to water.

"Jack, this is the second time today you broke your promise to not make me cry."

"The promise is void if they're tears of joy." He kissed her as they danced and cheers went sounded around them.

"You can't keep kissing me like that. It makes me weak in the knees," Diane said with passion in her eyes.

"You just took vows to let me kiss you like that for the rest of our lives."

The song ended, but they remained on the dance floor in each other's arms. "I'm starting to rethink the open bar. Cooper and Noli seem to be trying to drink enough to break the bank."

"Don't worry, the bar tab is on Cooper tonight. He lost a bet."

"Do I even want to know?"

He shook his head.

When the song Jack and Diane came on it seemed like Jack's entire family was on the floor. Those that were still in their chairs were singing along. Diane's family looked perplexed as to how all these people knew this song they'd never heard. Every time Jack and Diane were said in the song there were clinks on glasses for them to kiss, which they gladly obliged.

The next song was the electric slide. All of Diane's family, both young and old rushed to the floor and began to move in unison. It was Jack's family's turn to look inquisitively as to how everyone knew the dance to a song they'd never heard. Both songs got played again. By the third rotation of the electric slide, the dance floor was packed as everyone had learned the dance. The next time Jack and Diane played, both the guests of the bride and the groom sang along and clinked their glasses vigorously each time the couple's names were sung.

The bouquet headed directly towards Noli, but she batted it away like a volleyball and one of Jack's cousins from down south caught it. When Jack threw the garter it headed towards Cooper. He stepped out the way making it land on Ryan, who'd been standing on the side with his hands in his pocket.

After posing with the bouquet catcher, Ryan went to the bar for a drink. Amara came to stand next to him.

"You know only single men are supposed to catch the garter."

"I wasn't trying to catch it, and I didn't think it appropriate to announce my secret marriage at my sister's wedding."

"There would be no secret wedding if you signed the annulment papers," Amara said with narrowed eyes.

"Can I buy you a drink?"

"It's an open bar and you're trying to change the subject."

"I'm not going to discuss an annulment because I don't want us to end," Ryan said studying Amara's face for a reaction.

"What us? The only us that exists is you're Diane's brother and I'm her best friend. Other than that, there is no longer an us because you already put an end to it."

"There is to me. I screwed up, I know, but..." he trailed off when Diane joined them.

"Why do you two keep getting quiet every time I get near?"

"I was just telling your brother that I felt a migraine coming on." She shot him a look to ensure he wouldn't contradict her. "You look so beautiful Diane. And as strange as it sounds, I'm glad you were stranded on the side of the road. I'm really happy for you and Jack."

"Thank you. You should go lie down. Ryan can take you to the hotel?"

"No, I don't want him to." Diane raised an eyebrow at Amara's aggressive tone. "I mean I don't need him to, I can drive myself. I love you Diane. Congratulations." She kissed her friend on the cheek and left.

Once her best friend was safely out earshot, Diane said, "Ryan, you know if I had to choose between you and her that I'd choose her."

"There is not a doubt in my mind," Ryan said still staring at Amara.

"Then fix whatever this is so I won't have to choose."

"I'm trying."

"Good, now come dance with your sister."

Lena Hampton

SOCIAL NETWORK

Diane Sloan's relationship status is now married.
Jack Sloan's relationship status is now married.

chapter 16

.

D IANE AND JACK SAT IN the truck after the wedding headed to a cabin he'd rented in Kentucky.

"Are we there yet?"

"No, darling."

"I wish we'd chosen some place closer."

He smiled. "I'm excited too, darling."

"I'm excited, but I'm so tired I don't know if I'll be able to act on that excitement. For the past couple of months I've been practically attacking you. I'm like some addict that can only think of when I'm going to get my next touch or kiss from you, but right now I just want a nap."

"You can have me as much as you want for the rest of your life, so if we just sleep tonight it'll be okay. Or you can just take a nap now."

She yawned. "I want to keep you company while you drive." A couple of miles down the road she fell asleep. He didn't wake her until they reached the cabin that was isolated by thick tall trees and had a stream in the back. Diane went to the bathroom to change. Jack brought the bags in, unpacking some of the perishable foods, and started a fire.

When he walked into the bedroom, he stopped in his tracks. Diane was lying on the bed with only a sheer camisole and matching panties on. Her breasts were full and peeped out of the top. The darkness of her areola was visible through the transparent fabric. The white fabric enhanced her smooth rich brown skin. Her nervous smile made her even sexier.

"Wow."

"Thank you." she said smoothing out the fabric.

He wished that was his hand. He walked over to her and kissed her lips. "I love you. Let me change and I'll be right back."

"Let me help you." She said kneeling on the bed in front of him on the bed. He stood with his hands by his side. She started by undoing his tie, then concentrated on each button with shaky hands. His shirt fell to the floor and she rubbed her hands down his t-shirt clad chest until it reached the hem then she put her hands against his bare chest leaving her thumb hooked on the outside. Her hands inched their way up his muscled abdomen pulling his t-shirt up along the way. He snatched the t-shirt the rest of the way off and threw it to the floor, but it didn't speed up her hands leisure caress. Her fingers traced the trail of hair on his stomach moving closer to the waistband of his pants.

As her hands reached his belt he put his hands on her waist and pulled her in.

"Do you know what you're doing to me?" She raised her eyebrow with a coy smile on her face. The passionate look in her eyes drove him to cover her mouth with his. He held her closer and she threaded her hands into his hair. His hands caressed down her back, when his hands reached her round bottom he realized that she was wearing a thong. His large hands molded to its warm flesh. For months, he had fantasized about holding her like this and touching her everywhere and not having to control himself and stop. Tonight he wouldn't have to.

LATE THE NEXT MORNING sunlight streamed through the window onto the bed. The sheets were tangled around their bodies. Diane's head lay on his bare chest with a leg draped over one of Jack's. His arm was wrapped around her. The bright sun on her face prompted Diane to open her eyes. Lazily she began to run her fingers over his chest as she thought about how incredible it was to make love to her husband.

Jack laced his fingers through hers and brought her hand to his mouth for a kiss. "Darlin', I need a little more time to rebuild my energy after last night."

"One energy building breakfast coming up." She picked his shirt up off the floor and slipped it on.

Diane's bare feet walked across the wooden floor of the cabin's living room towards the kitchen. The floor was somewhat cold because the fire had gone out hours ago. She hummed as she opened the refrigerator and rummaged through bags, collecting the ingredients for pancakes and eggs. The aroma of fresh pancakes beckoned Jack into the kitchen. He stood in the entrance to the room wearing only navy boxers. His eyes were navigating her body. She turned to him and smiled. Her lips were soft and full and needed to be kissed.

His eyes revealed just how much he wanted her, but more importantly they showed how much he loved her. His boxers confined his desire, but that did not make it any less obvious. Looking at her thighs prompted him to move forward. He began by kissing her on the spot on the side of her neck that always elicited a moan.

"I thought you needed to rest and get your energy up."

"Seeing my beautiful wife standing in my shirt, cooking breakfast gave me energy."

"Since I've cooked, you will eat!"

"Will you feed me? In bed?"

"You can eat off of me if you want."

"Oh I want."

AS THEIR HONEYMOON WEEK was coming to an end, they managed to leave the cabin and enjoy the landscape and some shopping. One of their stops was in a bookstore. She found a book that interested her and pulled out her e-reader to purchase it while they stood in line at the store's café.

"Hi, what can I get for you?" the barista asked.

"I'll have a large black coffee," Jack said.

"A large house blend," the barista rephrased as he pushed keys on the register. "That will be $2.50."

Jack reigned in his irritation at the barista's rudeness for not taking Diane's order. He turned to Diane and said, "Darling, what do you want?"

She looked up from the e-reader. "A venti chai," she said returning her attention to the device.

"Sorry, I did not realize you two were together," the barista apologized sincerely. "One large black coffee and one large chai. Is there anything else?" he asked glancing at the person behind them in line before returning his gaze to Jack's perturbed eyes.

"Yes, one of those carrot cake cupcakes and a slice of chocolate cheesecake," Diane added.

"First name?"

"Jack." He got his change.

"Aren't you going to get anything to eat?" Diane asked.

Jack bent down with his mouth almost touching her ear. "You're going to share your goodies with me," he said softly with a wink. He kissed her cheek. He did not have to see her skin go flush with color to know she was blushing at the double entendre, it showed in her eyes. He took her hand into his as they found a seat.

They sat across from each other at the small wrought iron bistro table sipping on overpriced beverages and enjoying the sweet treats she'd ordered. He was flipping through AR Rifleman while she was immersed in the beginning chapters of the latest Sue Grafton novel.

"That didn't bother you?" Jack asked.

"What didn't bother me?" she responded confused.

"The cashier ignoring you."

"I didn't think he ignored me."

"He didn't acknowledge we were together."

"It's an understandable enough mistake," she said dismissing the thought with a flip of her hand.

"It's not understandable to assume we're not together because we're different races."

"I think it's more you're John Deere and I'm Prada, than the black and white thing. You're all down home country charm and I'm city slicker. I think it's pretty understandable to not assume we're together."

"We're too opposite to be together?"

"Not at all. I'm just saying that at first glance, we may not look like a couple." She reached across the table and put her hand on his. "We're like two puzzle pieces, it's our differences that make us fit together perfectly."

He slid his hand up her arm, and drew small circles with his thumb in the fold of her elbow then slowly caressed his way back to her hand. "We do fit together perfectly. You want to go back to the cabin and prove how well we fit together?" She bit her lip in anticipation and nodded.

They were a great fit, but how long would it be before his country ways ceased to be charming. He wondered if he could keep her happy enough that she wouldn't regret living in his world. He had his doubts that he could, especially since he didn't even know who or what Prada was. He hoped it wouldn't matter and, like his parents, the honeymoon would never have to end.

JACK KNEW THE HONEYMOON was over as soon as he saw Misti standing at the table with a smile on her face. Her joy was usually bad news for him. Diane was smiling at Misti but cut him a look that ripped out a part of his soul. He knew the smile was just for show. Diane would rather die than to let Misti know she'd gotten the better of her.

"Misti, what are you doing here?" Jack said with more than a hint of aggressiveness in his voice.

"I was just asking Diane here if she was helping you figure out the custody and child support for our baby," she said venomously sweet.

Jack moved his hand over his face to calm himself. "We don't know that that's my baby. And if it is that's something you should discuss with me and not my wife."

Diane remained quiet as her face grew more and more expressionless. Jack feared what was going on in her mind.

"I know you have your doubts about that night, but I don't. Jack I know this is your baby." She rubbed her stomach as she spoke to emphasize its swell. "Why can't I talk to Diane about it? I want to get to know our baby's stepmother better."

"Misti, you should go now," Jack said seeing Diane's hand tense and relax around the bottle neck.

"But Jack, we've been dancing around this for months. Why not discuss it now. The baby will be here sooner than you know."

Diane stood calmly. "If she doesn't want to leave, I do."

"Oh I get it," Misti said with a look of triumph on her face. "You hadn't told her about our baby yet?"

Jack did not respond. He threw a few bills on the table to cover the tab and followed Diane who was already leaving out the door. She was waiting at the truck's passenger side door when he walked out. He walked behind her to open the door and help her in as usual.

"I don't need any help," she bit out.

Jack waited to be sure she didn't. The height of the truck usually gave her trouble getting in and out, but fueled by simmering anger she hopped in with ease. Jack went to his side and got in, briefly praying that this would all work out somehow and berating himself for not having told her sooner. He started the truck and began to drive silently. He wanted her to take the lead on this conversation so he could gauge the exact temperature of her anger.

A few minutes into the drive she finally spoke. She stared directly out the window, not able to stomach looking at him and asked, "How far along is she?"

"About seven months." He knew she was doing mental calculations. "If I'm the father, it happened about a month before I met you."

"How long have you known?"

"Since the bachelor party."

She let out a sound that was somewhere in between a gasp and a sob and let the tears that had been collecting in her eyes fall.

"Di, I..."

She shook a hand in his direction for him to stop. "Jack I don't want to hear why you lied to me as you were confessing your love and honesty at our wedding."

"Di, I didn't lie to you."

"You did Jack. You said you'd never keep a secret from me and this is a doozie of a secret."

"I wasn't trying to keep this secret from you Di. I didn't want to bring into our marriage something that I didn't believe to be true. I have very little memory of the night that she claims we conceived. It was a Halloween party and just that morning we'd found out Dad was out of remission. I drank a little more than I should have and can only remember waking up the next morning in my bed."

"Then why not tell me that?"

"Because I didn't think you'd react well to it."

"When were you planning on telling me?"

"When I had confirmed that it was mine."

"If the baby turned out to be yours were you just going to come home with a baby one day and say surprise it's my turn for visitation? Or were you hoping the baby wasn't yours so you'd just never have to tell me?"

"It's not just hope, I really don't believe that baby is mine. I was drunk, but I could never be drunk enough to sleep with Misti."

"Whether or not the baby is yours isn't the biggest issue, the fact that you kept the possibility from me is. You promised you wouldn't keep things from me."

They were now parked in front of the house. He reached over to take her hand and she pulled away. "I'm sorry. I know that doesn't fix things. We were so happy that I didn't want anything to mess it up, especially unnecessarily."

She stared out the window. Her right hand played with the wedding rings on her left hand. "Perhaps I let my hormones make decisions instead of using rationality," she said more to herself than to him. "Maybe we moved too fast into such a permanent situation."

Jack gripped the steering wheel until his knuckles turned white. "Are you saying you wish we hadn't gotten married? That this should have just been a fling but we took it too far."

"I didn't say that Jack. Maybe we moved into this too quickly without thinking it all through."

"We or you? I know you thought you were the novelty and I'd move on once I got my fill, but now I see I should have been the one with that concern. You've had your fun with the white boy on the farm, but you've had enough and I've given you a way out that doesn't make you lose face."

"How is this my fault? You kept Misti having your baby from me! What other secrets are you keeping?"

"Diane, get off your high horse and stop acting like I'm the only one keeping secrets. You don't think that I know you've applied to every law firm in Chicago? Or that your visit to see your brother was actually your interviews?"

She looked at him for the first time since the restaurant. "What makes you think I've interviewed in Chicago?"

"I don't think it, I know it. I saw the emails with my own two eyes."

"How did you see that email? Are you spying on me?"

"A person without secrets can't be spied on. I saw it the day you told me to review the application for organic certification. You must have forgotten your email was still open. I also saw you had an entire folder of applications and responses with only one being within a hundred miles of here."

"I applied to see if I could get hired. It was never my intention to accept any of those positions. I just wanted to see if I was good enough."

"Diane, don't lie to me or yourself. This was about your friends moving on to these glamorous jobs and you regretting being stuck in the sticks with some hick."

"I've never said that."

"Not saying it and not feeling it are two different things. Diane, if you want to go, go, but don't use Misti's lies as your excuse. If I'm a mistake, say so."

Diane did not say anything. He had hoped for a blatant denial of her wanting to go, but did not get that. He looked at her face and only saw confusion. It was his turn to not be able to look at her.

"It's late and we're tired. We should go to bed and discuss it after we've had time to think," he said.

She slept in the guest room she used to sleep in, leaving him alone in their room. Neither of them got much sleep. She was up early the next morning in the kitchen fixing coffee when he walked in fully dressed for the day ahead. He walked behind her wrapped his arms around her.

"I missed you so much last night." She remained stiff in his arms.

"I think maybe I should go and spend time at my parent's and clear my mind. That'll give time for the paternity of Misti's baby to be determined."

He stepped back as though she'd just stabbed him.

"It'll be pretty difficult to work things out with you hundreds of miles away. Would this be a temporary living arrangement?"

She looked down at her hands. "I don't know."

"I don't think you leaving is what's best for our marriage. If you want to go, Diane, go. But I don't know how welcomed back you'll be."

"If I go to sort out my feelings it's over?"

"What feelings do you have to sort out Diane? Have I screwed up? Yes. Is it unforgivable? Not if you love me. You either love me and want to be with me or you don't."

"There is more to it than that."

"One night of you two doors down instead of by my side and I knew which one I wanted. I knew I wanted to do whatever needed to be done to be with you."

"If you're willing to do whatever then give me some time."

"If you don't love me enough to know that you want me, absence isn't going to make your heart grow fonder. Don't kid me or yourself. If you go home you won't be back."

"This is my home. If I come back will I be welcomed?"

"If you're going to go will you do me a favor and be gone before I return at the end of the day?" he left the house.

"I saw your bags in your car. I thought I asked you to be gone if you were going."

Diane had never seen Jack's eyes so ice cold. "I didn't want us to say goodbye like that."

"I don't want us to say goodbye. We can't always get what we want."

"Jack, I love you."

"Diane, don't. Don't give me hope. Please, just go." He turned to her and she saw tears in his eyes. She walked towards him to comfort him but he turned and walked back out the house.

Social Network

DIANE SLOAN'S STATUS: I'm confused, so very confused.

chapter 17

"HELLO?"

"Hi Jack," Diane said hopeful that this time he would talk to her and not just hang up. Sometimes Diane would call just to hear his voice say the two syllable greeting. She'd never meant for this to be the end of them, but things were more black and white for him. Her decision to take a break was viewed as her decision to leave him and he'd not spoken to her in those three months.

There was silence, but no dial tone.

"It's about your organic certification," she added before he hung up.

"I don't need you to handle that for me anymore. I'll text you the attorney's information and you can forward what you've done to him. Be sure to include your hours in it so I can pay you."

"I know you don't need me to do it but I want to do this for you Jack."

"I don't want you to do it. And please stop calling."

"I miss you Jack."

His response was slamming the phone down, but it did not hang up. She heard muffled voices in the background and then the sound of the phone being picked up followed shortly by the door slamming.

"Hi Diane."

"Hi Momma."

"Listen Diane. You know I love you, but Jack's my son. Please stop torturing him."

"I'm not torturing him. I just need to talk to him."

"About what? Are you coming back?"

"I don't know. I need to talk with him. I need to know if that's what he wants."

"Of course it's what he wants."

"If that's what he wants, why doesn't he even talk to me?"

"Because he's been miserable since you've left. The only thing he wants is you, not you on a phone, but you here with him. You need to decide if you want to come back and just do it. If you're not coming back, stop calling him so he has a chance to heal."

A COUPLE OF EVENINGS later Diane returned to her parent's house to see an overnight envelope addressed to her. She sat at the kitchen table with papers in her hand and an open overnight envelope on the table. The tears had dried, leaving salty white trails down her face.

"Diane, what are you doing here?"

"I live here."

"I know. What I do not know is why you are here when your heart is on a farm in southern Indiana."

She thought she saw concern on her Mother's face and heard a comforting tone in her voice. Diane let the tears fall she usually reserved for moments alone in her room at night.

"My broken heart is there."

"Why is your heart broken?"

"Because he lied to me mother and these came today."

Diane slid the papers across the table. Catherine took the papers from her daughter and read over them briefly.

"Yes, he lied to you. He will probably lie again. That is something people do. He doesn't really want this," she said raising the papers, "and neither do you. I was at your wedding and I remember something about loving through turmoil in your vows, not running when the turmoil comes along. He sent these papers because you left him, not because he does not love you."

"Why are you defending what he did? You don't even like him, Mother."

"I do not dislike him Diane. I am not defending what he did. He loves you. I did not think so at first, but now even I can see he does. He should have told you but he failed to, does that mean your marriage should end?"

"Why can't you just be on my side for once?"

"I am on your side. I have always been on your side."

"Really? You're always on my side? You were on my side through the whole ordeal with Alan? I'm sorry, I don't see how constantly pressuring me to work things out with him was being on my side. I especially don't see how inviting him to Jack's and my rehearsal dinner was you being on my side."

"I did those things because I thought you were making a mistake with Jack. I was trying to protect you from getting hurt. I thought you would be happier with Alan."

"Alan cheated! How could he be better?"

"Did you really expect him to be celibate for four years Diane?"

"I never loved him enough to give myself to him. I didn't love him at all. I was only with him because I thought it would make you happy. I thought you'd be proud of me and finally love me."

Catherine gasped. "Diane, you don't think I love you?"

"I think you only love me because you're my Mother and it's the proper thing to do. I am not nearly perfect enough in your eyes for you to love just because. If you don't want me here you don't have to try and get me to go back to Jack. I'll leave so you don't have to be reminded how miserably I've failed."

Diane wiped at the fresh tears on her face and started out of the room. She stopped when she heard what sounded like a sob come from her mother. When she turned she was shocked to see her mother with tears running down her face and her hand over her mouth muffling her weeps. She stood frozen with her tear filled eyes locked with her mother's watery ones. She had never seen her mother shed a single tear, let alone let them pour out and risk her mascara running. Her mother was not a pretty crier.

"Diane, I could not love you more than I do. I thought you knew."

"How am I supposed to know when you are always so critical of me?" The fight had gone out of Diane's tone.

"I am so proud of you. You are perfect to me. I want so much for your life to be perfect because I love you so much. I have never meant to be critical. I have only tried to guide you."

"If you want my life to be perfect, why were you pushing me to Alan?"

"I thought you loved him. I thought he made you happy."

"I love Jack, but you tried so hard to break us up. Why?"

Catherine took a deep breath and looked around before she began to speak. She moved until she was standing right in front of her daughter. She lowered her voice to a barely audible whisper.

"There was someone before your father. I'll call him Sam. I was head over heels in love with him. He hung the moon and placed every star." Her mother's voice did not sound as though these were memories she revered, but a past she was retelling with a pang of regret.

"I thought he felt the same way about me, but he did not, far from it. Like Jack, he was white." Diane's eyes widened with shock. "He was from one of those 'villes downstate with no blacks. He said and did everything just right for me to give him the one thing I could never get back. Shortly thereafter he decided he could not be in a long term relationship with a black girl. Marriage was certainly out of the question. He said he needed someone who was 'more appropriate for his aspirations'."

"I'm so sorry."

"I was devastated. I lost more weight than was healthy and my grades suffered horribly. That's when I met your father. He was my tutor. He helped me pull my grades and myself back together. He did not sweep me off my feet in another whirlwind romance, but he took my hand and slowly guided me to a lasting love."

Diane understood now. She remembered back to her mother's words during the drive to the farm on the unplanned trip. "You thought Jack was like Sam and Alan was like dad. You thought I'd regret being with Jack."

"Yes. I was projecting my past onto your present. Do you forgive me?"

"Of course I do."

"Good." She hugged her daughter tightly. "I love you Diane."

"I know now. I love you too."

Catherine ended the embrace and held Diane's face in her hands. "You love Jack and he loves you. If that baby is his, that's something you will need to face together. You need to forgive him, not for his sake, but because you are not happy without him."

"Ma, I miss him so much."

Ma sounded so much more affectionate than mother and Catherine liked it. "You do not have to miss him anymore."

"You're right." Diane kissed her mother on the cheek and headed towards the door.

"Where are you going?"

"Home."

"Good, but you should fix your face before you go. You look a fright."

"If I look a fright, you look a horror." They both laughed. Diane liked the direction her relationship was heading with her mother. They'd laughed and cried together for the first time ever this afternoon. More importantly, they understood each other better.

Social Network

Diane Sloan's status: I'm nervous, so very nervous.

chapter 18

"HI JACK, DON'T HANG UP. I need your help," Diane rushed out in one breath.

Jack closed his eyes and silently sighed. Every time he heard her voice he felt the sweet swell of hope and the bitter plunge of despair. He knew he shouldn't answer her calls, but he craved the sound of her voice saying his name.

"What do you need help with?" He kept his voice neutral and void of desire.

"My car has stopped. Can you come get me?"

"Diane, it would be quicker if you called AAA. They'd make it to you long before I made it to Gary."

"I'm not in Gary. I'm somewhere on the road between Bloomington and the farm. It's dark, I'm surrounded by corn, and I'm scared."

Jack's heart began to race. Was she coming back or was she bringing the divorce papers and piercing his heart by putting the final nail in their marriage's coffin. If she was coming back he'd want to take her in his arms and kiss her breathless. If she had the divorce papers, he'd want to take her in his arms and kiss her senseless to convince her to stay.

"I'll be there in a few."

The entire way to her he sent up prayers that she was coming back home. He couldn't wait to see her but also didn't think he could stomach seeing her again. Life had been miserable since she left, but he wanted her to be happy, even if it wasn't with him. He really wished she could be happy with him.

When he finally caught sight of her car, a huge case of nerves hit him. He turned the truck around so that it was directly behind her car. Instead of going to her window he walked to the front of the car and motioned for her to pop the hood. She followed his instructions then got out of the car. She was standing close enough that he could smell her perfume in the breeze.

"Thank you for coming, Jack."

"No problem," he said, examining under the hood with a flashlight, afraid to look at her for fear of what he might see in her eyes.

"It's good to see you."

"Is it?" he said, still studying the car's inner workings.

She stepped closer and put her soft hand on his stubble roughened chin, gently turning him towards her. "Whatever is wrong with the car can be handled tomorrow."

Jack studied her face in the glow from his headlights. "Why are you here?"

"Your Mom said you still love me and that you wanted me back if I wanted to come back. Is that true? Do you want me back?"

"Do you want to come back?"

"Yes."

"Are you sure? I can't take it if you change your mind again."

"I'm sure. I love you. These have been the most miserable months of my life." Tears welled up in her eyes. "Especially when I got the divorce papers." Tears began to stream down her face.

Jack wiped the tears away. "You promised you'd never cry again." He claimed her mouth, moving his hands to her waist and pulling her close. When he heard the soft moan he'd missed so much over the last few months he picked her up and carried her to his truck. He drove the short distance home at a breakneck pace.

"GOOD MORNING," SHE said trying to avoid assaulting him with her morning breath. He pinched her upper thigh. "Oww. What was that for?"

"I wanted to make sure you were really here and not just a dream."

"You're supposed to pinch yourself."

"I like pinching you better," he said with a chuckle.

She sat up in the bed, making sure to cover her body with the sheet. "Last night, we got distracted and really didn't get to talk about the things that came between us."

"You're right." He sat up too. "I know you think you won't have a career here, but I was thinking. I did a lot of thinking about you while you were gone."

"I was thinking about you too. I was more hoping that you didn't hate me. You wouldn't talk to me and I thought it was because you hated me and didn't want me anymore."

"If I talked to you there was a good chance I'd be in jail for kidnapping. Hearing your voice made me want to tie you up and bring you back here against your will."

"Is it wrong that I'm kind of turned on by that?"

"Only if it's wrong that it turns me on that that turns you on."

"You said you were thinking about my career?" She asked, getting them back on task.

"Well, I was thinking about all the advice and help you've given. Like helping with the transfer of the farm and Cooper mentioned you helping him with some contracts."

"How much business is it like that, and how many of the people around here are going to come to me."

"You saw the turnout at our wedding."

"That's because word got out it was an open bar."

He laughed. "That was part of it, but most of them were there for us. They were happy for me because they like you so much. Most people blame me for you leaving.

I've talked with a lot of people and they want you to take them on as clients. I was thinking you can start in the house and as you get more clients we can rent an office in Bloomington."

"Or I can go work at a small firm there. One of my professors is a partner and was excited to get my call this afternoon. I'm supposed to have lunch with her and her partner later in the week."

"I wish there was a way for you to have your big city firm and be here with me."

"I don't. I don't feel that I'm giving anything up by being right here. I experienced the big city firm and I didn't like it. In fact I hated it. I was just a very small cog in a giant machine."

"At least now you won't wonder about the road not taken."

"True." She took a deep breath, "I did some thinking about the Misti issue."

"About that-"

"Listen, I love you," she continued before he could speak. "If being a stepmother is part of the package, I'll be the best stepmother I can be. With Misti for a mother the child will need all the help it can get."

"Do you really mean that?"

"Yes."

"How did I get so lucky?" he asked, pulling her close.

"I drive a foreign car."

"You won't be a stepmother. The baby's not mine. Trevor, one of the bartenders at Cooper's place said he drove me home Halloween night. She was already pregnant that night anyway."

"I'm sorry I ran. I won't do that again. It was just all so overwhelming and I didn't deal with it as well as I could have."

"I should have told you about Misti sooner."

"I should have told you about the applications and interviews."

"We can't keep things from each other. We have to be honest about everything, including our feelings."

She let the sheet fall to her waist. "I feel like making up for lost time."

Social Network

Diane Sloan's status: I'm happy, so very happy.

Jack Sloan's status: I'm happy too, so very happy.

epilogue

"HEY DARLING, WHAT ARE YOU doing home early?" Jack asked one afternoon several weeks after Diane had returned to the farm.

"A girl can't come home for lunch?"

"Not if that girl expects to get back to work," he said pulling her in for a kiss.

She broke the kiss as his hand started to caress her body. "I came home because I need to talk to you."

He looked at her seriously. "What's wrong Di?"

"Well, you know how we agreed that I'd get my career started before we had any children?" Diane asked

"Yeah. I'm fine with that. Did you get a job offer you couldn't refuse?"

"You could say that."

"Where is it? How far away?" He mentally braced himself for her response. "If this is what you want we can make it work. We will make it work."

She smiled. "It's really close."

"Good because I'd like to make love to my wife more than once a month. What is this offer?"

"It's not just an offer, I already accepted."

"I thought we agreed that we'd make these big decisions together."

"This one was kind of made for us. Remember when I came back home and you carried me to the truck, then to the bed that we didn't leave much for the entire day?"

"Oh, yes." He put his hands on her waist thinking of re-enacting that day.

She moved his hands and placed them on her stomach. "Well one of those times we made love worked."

"Worked? Are you saying you're pregnant?"

"We're pregnant," she corrected.

"Are you sure?"

She pulled the sandwich bag holding the pregnancy test out of her pocket. "Positive. It says so right there."

He looked into her eyes. "Are you happy about this?"

"So happy. I can't begin to tell you how happy I am."

"You're not going back to work today."

"I hadn't planned on it."

JACK 8 DIANE

acknowledgments

First and foremost I want to thank God for giving me the gift to create stories and characters. It took me a while to stop hiding my candle under a bushel. Now I'm letting it shine and hopefully reflecting You in my writing.

I also want to acknowledge myself. Not in the conceited "I did this all by myself" way but in the "I'm shocked I finally completed a novel after all these years" way. Over the last couple of decades, I'd accumulated countless character profiles, outlines, first chapters, and other various parts of books without finishing a single one. As one of my friends so aptly put it, this has been a long time coming.

The two people I hold most responsible for me finally completing this work are Michele Kimbrough and Chris

Baty. Michele is my cousin. One day in 2011, probably about October 22nd, she asked on Facebook who else was going to participate in National Novel Writing Month (NaNoWriMo). I clicked the link and saw that it was a 30-day 50,000 word challenge. It sounded crazy. I like crazy, I do it very well. Chris Baty is the person who started the insanity that is NaNoWriMo. His idea to challenge writers to just write until they get to 50K words made me chain and duct tape my self-editor in the locked basement of my mind until I got to the end. I truly believe Jack and Diane would still be a mere idea and a few disorganized plot notes if I was not determined to win the challenge.

Michele did more than make me aware of the challenge. She also provided support in the form of weekly video chats. We bounced around ideas about our novels and encouraged each other during the month of NaNoWriMo. The video chats didn't stop. It was her continued support and faith in my storytelling skills that made me go forth with not just finishing a novel, but getting it out there in the world.

My children also deserve thanks, too. I was constantly telling them to use their gifts. This fell under the do as I say, not as I do category of parenting. I know that parenting by example is a much better way to get the message across, so I took my own advice. I wanted to show them that they can do anything they put their minds to because I did.

On that same note, thanks to my sister Angee and my mother Mary. They are extremely creative and talented, and I've been trying to get them to put their ideas and art out into the world for years. Me finally sharing my talents has spoken more to them than any of my talking ever did. They have been amongst my biggest supporters and champions throughout the entire process.

Thanks to all those who helped polish my rough draft into a diamond (or at least a CZ) by reading and critiquing my work. My sister Angee, understood exactly who I had in mind as I wrote Catherine. My friend Carlton helped me with the male perspective and much more. Thanks to my proofreader Jenn for finding inconsistencies and her other valuable comments that let me know when I was on the right path or when I was out in the woods. Once again, thanks to Michele for her countless reads during every stage of the book and turning it into a page turner.

Thanks to all those who have said they were proud of me or are just as excited as I am about this. Your encouragement is priceless.

Thanks to Art Fry (inventor of the Post-It Note) for making my ideas and random dialogue stick around (sorry I'm not sorry for the pun) long enough to make it onto the page. Even these acknowledgments started on his invention.

a note from the author

Thank you so much for reading my book! I hope you enjoyed reading it as much as I enjoyed telling it. If you did enjoy it, please leave a review. Even a short review is a great way to support me and help others enjoy Jack and Diane's story.

Love,
Lena

Find Lena across the web:

Website: indewstyle.com
Email: dew@indewstyle.com
Instagram: indewstyle

also by Lena Hampton

Someone to Love

She's afraid of love and he doesn't believe in it.

Magnolia Freeman travels the world trying to outrun the pain of her parents' sudden deaths. As much as Magnolia dreads returning home she can't deny her favorite cousin's requests to help plan her wedding.

Cooper Smith believes no good can come from love. As far as he's concerned a "relationship" shouldn't last more than a night—or two nights if it's a holiday weekend. Despite his skepticism about love, he volunteers his restaurant for his best friend's wedding.

Magnolia and Cooper give in to their attraction since neither of them are looking for anything serious. When their fling turns into something more Magnolia leaves but can't get the heartbroken Cooper out of her mind or her heart, especially when there's a permanent reminder of him growing inside her.

Can Magnolia and Cooper get beyond their fears to find someone to love?

The Nearness of You

Their marriage was over before it began.

Newlywed Amara's heart is shattered into dust when her groom destroys her career as a political advisor to advance his own as an investigative journalist. Despite loving him she leaves without a word.

Ryan has no choice but to break the news story about Amara's senator boss on national TV without warning her, but he never gets the chance to explain. Amara is the only woman he's ever loved. He is determined to make their marriage work.

He agrees to dissolve the marriage on the stipulation they live as husband and wife first. It is difficult for Amara to continue to deny her feelings for Ryan when he's shirtless in the morning handing her a mug of life-sustaining coffee. Just as their nearness puts their happily ever after in reach history repeats itself when Ryan discovers a secret about Amara's new boss.

Is their love strong enough to last forever?

other titles from inDEWstyle

Whiskey Kisses by Dan Elizabeth

A wild celebrity meets a serene accountant.

Wilder Mann is accustomed to sneaking out on groupies before they wake up, not chasing them down the hotel hall barefoot in his boxers to keep them from leaving with a part of his heart. Then again, Serenity is no groupie. She's not even a fan.

Despite her best efforts Serenity Breedlove can't resist Wilder's charm and falls for the caring and vulnerable man behind the country singer's bad-boy swagger. But she learns dating a star has its pitfalls when her weight becomes the topic of national discussion. While Serenity loves Wilder the man, she is not a fan of Wilder the persona.

Can their love survive his fame?

Made in the USA
Columbia, SC
01 November 2024